The Bread of Life

This edition published 2026
by Living Book Press

ISBN: 978-1-76153-872-8 (hardcover)
         978-1-76153-877-3 (softcover)

First published in 1910.

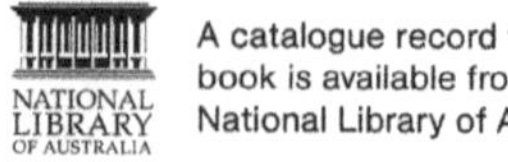

The Saviour of the World

Book 4

The Bread of Life

by

Charlotte M. Mason

Contents

The Last Supper

Leonardo da Vinci

Introductory Note

By the Rev. WM. H. DRAPER, M.A.,
Rector of Adel

IN times of intellectual stress and change, when the progress of knowledge and criticism compels every thoughtful reader to see old truths from new points of view, there are some people to whom the point of view of Poetry seems to afford a prospect not otherwise obtainable, and therefore that it is worth taking up, at least tentatively, in spite of the difficulty of making the foothold secure.

The reason for so considering the point of view of Poetry is that it stands clear of the dust of controversy. Those who look from it know that they cannot see detail, cannot make out exact definitions, but can see form, the outline of which is softened by distance; and mass, the colour of which is enriched and toned by intervening space and air.

What is the relative value of this point of view, on the subject here treated, cannot yet be finally determined. But no vindication is needed of the wisdom of the idea that it is worth trying. To employ it is like the action of stepping a little further from a picture when our present position seems to show something too hard or disproportioned in the outlines or too strong in the light. One might even say more than this and affirm that the use of poetry is the use of a different light, namely, that of imagination; demanding rare skill in its gradations, but, when handled according to knowledge, promising new perceptions.

The writer of this little volume, part of a more extended

work which aims at giving some new perceptions over the field covered by the Evangelists' records, has adopted the medium of verse as the best way of explaining at once what her aim is. She is deeply aware of what may be said against such an attempt. She knows that the mere use of verse at all is taken by some as a kind of challenge. But when so taken it is, so far as she is concerned, mistaken. Verse is here chosen because it is the accepted instrument of poetry, and what is hjere said in verse is said from the Art's point of view. But her chief object has been not to make a poem but to illuminate a theme which is itself to her more than poetry and includes it because it is the Truth of all truths and the Life of all lives.

When familiarity with the letter of Scripture has thrown a kind of veil over the eyes, when critical and theological controversies have raised a dry dust round the Figures and scenes pourtrayed,-in such a time come the opportunity for poetry to describe what it sees in freshness of spiritual per-ception and in gazing back on the Past without controversy and from a heart at peace.

Whether the hand which holds the pen may sometimes tremble or no, and whether or not the skill of the artist be at times imperfect, yet, if the spirit of the art is there, it will awake in others those same new perceptions, a consciousness of which first moved the writer to take up the pen and then to go on with so great an endeavour, in which to fail is easy and to succeed is hard.

W.H.D.

Author's Note

I should like to acknowledge very gratefully my indebtedness to the Rev. W. H. Draper, not only for the exceptional insight his "Introductory Note" manifests, but for very valuable and sympathetic criticism on some part (Book I.) of the MSS. of this work. Any who have had the pleasure of hearing his Oxford University Extension Lectures on the Divina Commedia will be able to judge how competent a critic of poetry Mr. Draper is, and also how well-read a theologian.

CONTENTS OF VOLUME I

THE HOLY INFANCY

Angels and prophets long had searched in vain
Those mysteries, now, for wayfarers writ plain:

How Christ was born in Bethlehem of pure Maid,
How to three kings His Rising was displayed:

How holy Simeon blessed Him and foretold
His Mother's grief, He, sacrificed and sold.

How out of Egypt did God call His Son
That all the prophets figured might be done.

How, simple Child, He dwelt in Galilee
That simple folk His light might daily see.

How to Jerusalem in His twelfth year
He went, before Jehovah to appear:

How there He shed His light, a duteous Boy,
To keep the law His errand, not destroy.

How eighteen years of meek submission then
Prepared Him for His labours amongst men.

How He went out to John to be baptised,
And John in Him a greater recognised.

How in the wilderness for Forty Days
He bare assaults of Satan. Give we praise!

How in Caná He made the water wine,
That men should see of life in Him a sign.

How in Jerusalem quick drave He forth
The traders and their wares—of how small worth!

How journeying north to Galilee once more,
He sate and taught that Woman of heavenly lore.

How all the men came out who heard His fame,
And, SAVIOUR OF THE WORLD, did Him
    proclaim.

These things have we considered as we might,
And hence would meekly follow in His light.

CONTENTS OF VOLUME II

HIS DOMINION

Christ healed the rich man's son: the man believed;
"God is a spirit," the lesson he received.

He preaches to His own; mad hate they bring,—
Would from steep brow of hill the Saviour fling!

People who sat in darkness saw great light
Whose brightness baffled unaccustomed sight:

Those fishers four on Sea of Galilee
The fishers of the Lord were called to be:

At Capernaum Christ preached: the people heard,
And knew Authority was in His word.

Vile spirits bade He forth in that same hour,
And all men recognised an unknown Power.

Peter's wife's mother, raised from fevered bed—
By hand that raised her would thenceforth be led.

"At even ere the sun was set," they came
To Him for healing, sick and blind and lame.

Then wearied, He, a great while before day,
Went out to desert place that He might pray.

The folk of Galilee would make Him King;
He knows how little worth the praise they bring.

Weary with preaching, Christ bade put to sea;
Behold, a wondrous draught, the fishers' fee!

A leper cried, Thou canst,—wilt make me clean?
I will, saith Christ; healed, who had leprous been!

Levi took customs' dues by the seaside,
And when the Master called, he straight replied.

His Jews rejected for hypocrisy;
Too skilled in subterfuge, what hope have we?

Man at Bethesda's pool so long had lain—
The Lord who healed him to betray was fain!

Christ taught,—the Father and the Son were One
In words They spake, in all works They had done.

On the Son the royal crown of judgement set;—
He learned the ways of men, nor would forget;

In Him was Life; and all the souls that live
Draw breath from Him, to Him their praises give.

The Law, the prophets, witness; to each heart,
The Father testifies, and shows his part.

Thy Jews condemned, grant us, good Lord, to heed—
Unstable in our faith, slack in our deed!

Christ walked in cornfield on the Sabbath day,
And set men free from bondage whilst they pray.

He instantly the withered hand restores,
And, grieved, the Rulers' faithlessness deplores.

Once more to fair Genesareth He came,
And multitudes drew nigh, with love aflame.

Our Founder chose the Twelve, and laid them, sure
Stones to sustain that Church which shall endure.

He charged them; told them, how the poor are blest;
How persecutions should their lives molest:

Taught them the brother-secret; how to give;
How with all men as brothers they should live.

On blind man led by blind man, cupboard's store,
Of building House of Faith, He told them more:

And then He climbed the Mount that all might hear,—
That multitude had come from far and near:

"Blessed are they that mourn," He told the sad;—
With promise of the Father's care made glad.

Chaste must they be and kind and guard their speech;—
For God's own holiness is in man's reach.

He taught men how to give their alms, to pray;
And all their anxious fears to put away.

Behold, the Church He founded on that day
Received those Institutes should guide her Way.

The people heard, and hardly understood,
But knew the Word He spake was very good;

Perceived Authority in every word
And fain would bear due fruit of that they'd heard.

CONTENTS OF VOLUME III

THE KINGDOM OF HEAVEN

*The centurion, begging that the Lord would heal
His suffering servant, did great faith reveal.*

*Behold, with joy return the mourning train
Come forth to bury that young man of Nain.*

*The prisoner, John, makes question by his friends;
News of His works, the answer Jesus sends.*

*"What went ye to the wilderness to see?"
Cried Jesus, praising John's fidelity.*

*A woman anoints His feet with costly nard;
Christians shall know thy deed—her great reward.*

*He walks in Galilee, and women tend,
And gladly of their substance on Him spend.*

*The sower sowed in various kinds of ground;
The Lord to hearts of men a likeness found.*

Who knows the things of God and doth not tell,
Like him who hides a lamp, doth not do well.

Together are let grow the wheat and tares,
Till each kind to its place the reaper bears.

Thou think'st to watch the growing of the seed?
A secret, that,—so by God's will decreed.

A grain of mustard-seed, so small to see,
May yet become a mighty sheltering tree.

Thou'st found a treasure? Go and sell thine all,
Ere thou this treasure all thine own may'st call.

The woman hid the leaven in her flour;
The Word hid in a heart shall rise with power.

A merchant came upon a pearl of price
And forthwith bought—by liberal device.

And, "Have ye understood?" the Saviour cried;
"Yea, Lord," they said, but in their lives denied.

"Thy mother and Thy brethren would Thee see;"
"These be My kinsfolk—they follow Me."

Proud Nazareth rejected Him who came
To save the humble: Do not we the same?

Jesus came walking o'er the stormy sea;
His friends, relieved, were there—where they would be.

The demoniac raged as fierce as angry storm;
Christ spake,—and meek he sat who'd wrought such
    harm.

The little maid was raised by Jesus' hand:
"Now, see ye no man tell," the Lord's command.

A woman crept behind and healing took;
Christ made her happy by a pitying look.

Two blind men came and cried on Him for sight:
The Lord restored to these the joys of light.

A dumb deaf man sat moody by the way;—
Christ taught dumb lips to praise His name that day.

The time had come to send the Twelve abroad,—
Bless'd messengers to carry forth the Word.

As father charges son would cross the seas,
So Christ, their Father, gave His charge to these.

"Dangers I see await you on your way;—
Be prudent, friends, and bide a better day.

But have no fear; knows not your Father all
Of good or ill His children shall befal?

Yet ye must bear the cross, nor shrink in shame
From any obloquy or any blame.

Of this be sure, whoever you befriends,
Your Father in heaven will make that man amends."

Forth fared the Twelve in pairs to do His will,
And as they went, the Lord was with them still.

With joy these men returned to show their Lord
How it had prospered with the seed, His Word.

Now, John the Baptist prisoned in strong tower
To chide the king had used a prophet's power:

The king sware foolish oath to grant what boon
The princess asked of him; vindictive, soon—

"Give me John Baptist's head," she cried; and, lo,
The sorry king bade arméd men to go

And bring the prophet's head. The news was brought
To John's disciples; quick they Jesus sought

And told their grief to Him. "Come ye apart,"
Saith Christ to the weary Twelve; with tender heart

They follow Him and tell what things befel
In all the cities—whether ill or well

BOOK I

The Bread of Life

I

In a desert place

"Come ye apart to a desert place and rest,"
Saith Christ to His Chosen Twelve, returned to Him
From wanderings, healings, teachings, manifold.
But, see, the people will not be outdone,
Nor let their Lord, theirs also, out of sight!
They watched Him enter the boat with those, His
    friends;
Tumultuous, eager, followed they on foot
Round the head of the lake, heedless of noon-day
    heat;
Crowds gathered to them from the cities round,
And, lo, that desert place the Lord had sought—
Spot lovely and remembered, was't, perhaps,
For many a prayerful vigil, solitary,—
The crowd, iconoclast, had broke the spell,
Shattered that image of sweet solitude
Which refreshed the Master's thought! See,
    multitudes
Are there before Him, waiting for His words.

Men of sweet nature, sure, might feel annoy
At such rude trespass on hour set apart
For rest and converse with their chosen friends:
They of sweet nature, aye, but not the Christ:
Tender, He welcomed all these scattered sheep
Having no shepherd; diligently taught
Through all the long day things that concerned their
  peace—
Things of the Kingdom which was for each of them:
They heard with greedy ear: all learned that day,
That, whoso comes to Christ comes always well;
Never intrudes on secret communings,
Hears words for other ears, presumes on hours
Devoted to great matters; all's for him,
Poor wretch who has no claim!

II

"Jesus went up into the mountain"

He climbed the slope in sight of all the folk;
They watched, nor looked away, and knew at heart,
Unknowing that they knew, that in Him alone
Was all their hope, their life; without Him nought!
He sat with His disciples there; He spake
Of the Kingdom of God and how men enter in:
Of what, we know not save by gathering up
Words elsewhere He had uttered, other time;
By conceiving baffling thought of parables
And sayings precious, unregarded pearls,
That no man gathered for our after-use!

The time wore on; for many hours the folk,
A moved and swaying throng, gave heed to words
That Christ let fall among them. The day far spent,
The Disciples came to Him, urged common sense;
(Nay, sure, in this thing, they more wise than He!
So the crowd scores o'er poets and the rest,
Who top them by head and shoulders; they have
    sense!)
Sententious spake they, in dull human wise;

"See, here's a desert place, night's drawing on,
A great multitude's about with nought to eat,—
Forgetting hunger now, but by-and-by?—
Good Master, be advised: send them away
That they may lodge in villages at hand
And buy something to eat!" "What need that they
Should go away? give ye them bread to eat."
Were ever men of sense brought quicker up
Before th' impossible, preposterous!
All high things knew the Lord, but this small
     thing—
The people's supper, how to get them home,—
How should great minds descend to small concerns?
Their plan was good, but He must have His way,
And theirs, to abide the thing He willed to do!

III

A venture of faith

THE LORD sat wearied after day-long speech,
Passing of "virtue" from Him in those signs—
Compassionate miracles—He wrought for them.
The people looked and heard and took their fill
Of the life that was in Jesus. (Wherefore, then,
But a handful gathered in that upper room
To fulfil their last obedience, when multitudes,
Arrested by His signs, had paid that due—
Attention to His words—which should lead to life?
Alack, an active part was theirs to play:
'Tis not enough to feed—e'en on the Word:
To assimilate that we take is our concern,
Else, we go empty!)
Lifting up His eyes,—
He sees great multitudes have come to Him:
Ah, good for us that one was by who loved,
And garnered bread for Christendom's fond heart!
Blessed to know that, *there* He sat, our LORD;
Where lies the spot, we know not, but rejoice
With brooding mind to know that, on a place,
Here on our very earth, the Saviour sat!

21

Bless'd to know surely that He raised His eyes;—
Love treasures such things up; the love of John
Made record for us; our love tells her gains;
Surpassing reverence transports the heart
To note the Lord's regard, observe Him, sit!
And now the Master tests that growth in faith—
The disciples' sole concern, our only care:
One picks He out; turning to Philip, saith,
(Our testing finds us ever one by one!)
"Whence buy we bread that all these folk may eat?"
As when a King calls young knight to his side—
"Thou art a man of valour—kingly hest
I lay on thee; go do this valiant deed!"—
Was Philip honoured that day 'mongst his peers
With opportunity for splendid faith,
More in regard of Christ than any work!
Would we'd been there to answer, "Lord, I know
That Thou canst feed men, heal them, give them life!
Such chance was Philip's: but perceived he not
Himself, a school-boy called to say his task:
The lesson, is it conned? Go higher, thou;
But, stumblest in the saying? Go thou down;
So, Philip had his chance to praise the Lord!

By what perverseness harden we our heart
When friend makes meek appeal for sympathy
In noble purpose, soul-uplifting thought?
Then, practical are we; would count the cost,
Bid him beware of that generosity,
Or sneering men will ask, 'What hast in bank,

What coin or credit with the Highest?' So,
Did Philip answer, reckoning up the cost:
"Two hundred pennyworth of bread is not enough
To afford a little bread to each of these."—

Alas, for Philip! One chance, they say, men have,
One single chance for greatness in a life:
Philip lost his for common sordid thought—
What good's done on the earth, that, money does;
And, Were we rich, what great things would we do!

Another heard, one of a generous stock,
Whose brother cast his all on one great throw,
One lottery of faith,—Peter, who owned,
"Thou art the Christ of God!"—Now, Andrew saith,
"A lad's here with five loaves, two fishes small;"—
And in his heart he thought, "Enough for one,
May't in His hands feed all this numerous host?"
Sudden ashamed of his temerity, he adds—"But what
      are they
For all this multitude?" With failing heart,
He launched his petty bark, the "Little Faith":
Ah, were't an ocean vessel for this voyage!

IV

Christ our "Providence"

"Now make them all sit down:" and that same John,
Who splendours saw of the new Jerusalem,
The rainbow throne, the sardis, emerald,—
Here, also, saw what fed his artist-eye;—
Saw much grass in the place; the vivid-hued
Garments of eastern men amongst the flowers,—
Kaleidoscope of colours: soon, the word
Came, bidding all to sit by companies;
See, a score of open squares, with space in midst
Where Christ stood with th' disciples, and that
    meal—
That little meal which should sustain them all—
Mocking the eyes of thousand hungry folk
Thus bidden to break fast! Did any know
With soft assurance in his inward heart
That, the thing He gives sufficeth, less or more?

How good to us, anhungered, to perceive
The Master's mind disclosed in all the tale,
See order emanating from His act
As song from throat of throstle! so did John see

A jewelled glory as of painted glass
Reflected on his vision from the Christ's thought!—
How good to see our Saviour in the midst
Dealing out bread to all that multitude
E'en as He deals to us in harvest field!
The harvest's yellow glory in all lands,
In Egypt, Syria, distant western fields,
The table spread for us as for the birds,—
How this one scene interprets the Lord's ways!

Lo, that large circle, those five thousand souls,
Raised eyes to Him in their midst; He took the
    loaves,—
The little barley cakes, the fishes two,—
And, looking up to heaven, He blessed the meat
And gave God thanks Who feeds us. That poor
    "Grace"
We say before meat,—convicted, we elude
The eye of Him who taught us! Consider we
This feeding of five thousand, and we perceive
How the very life of God comes with our bread!
He brake the loaves and fishes, gave the meat
To the disciples, they to th' multitude:—
Behold, our uses! That He hands to us,
For distribution is't, that all may eat;
We, honoured in His service and in theirs.

The people ate accustomed fare with zest—
The wonder of 't! And ate the more to try,
Could the supply give out and any lack?

In time they were all filled; and the ordered mind
Of Him, the universe sustains and made,
Appeared in a little matter, "Gather up,"
Said He who fed them with unlaboured act,
"The broken pieces that none be lost."
No trifling thing, these fragments of men's food;—
Organic life alone can life sustain;
Cycles of time, processes manifold,
Initial act creative, evolving care
Of Him who first had made,—all these had gone
To make rejected crust, fragment of fish:
And those twelve baskets filled with broken meat,
Of God's world-providence tell the tale!

V

The people would make Him king

"Here's of a truth that Prophet of the Lord
Moses foretold should lead the folk like him,
Like him, give bread to spare in the wilderness!"
So spake all they who heard what Christ had done:
Full well they spake; who knows to open wide
Men's mouths with hunger, knows straightway to
    drop
Food that shall animate or fainting flesh,
Or heart sunk low in courage; to give new life
To all the failing goodness of a soul,—
He, Prophet of the World! the One who sees,—
Knows all the needs of men, and ministers!

"This Prophet be our King!" they cry them hoarse,
Allured by the hope of bread for men spread thick
As manna in the barren wilderness!
What need to labour? All should sit at ease;
His bread provided, each himself should please!
"Why, what's a King for but his people's bread
To furnish, liberal, constant: this is He!
Unwilling, He hangs back, but we are strong,

The many people, sure, may make their King!"
And hot, impetuous, by one impulse moved,
They came perforce to seize and make Him King!
The disciples stood exultant, from their eyes
Encouragement spake out; all the mad crowd
Knew them supported by these grave good men.

VI

The miracle of increase

THAT miracle of increase—what the steps,
And at what moment did the change take place?
Did broken fragments multiply the while—
The instant's space—they passed through Jesus'
   hands?
The Disciples' baskets—were they straightway filled
Direct from the hands of the Lord? Or, grew the
   store
In the act of giving, each portion leaving more
Than itself to fill its place? Idle, we ask;
Who tells us how the goodly grain is built,—
The seed, the blade, the ear, full corn in ear—
That man knows th' processes of miracles,
How thousands may be fed, how tempests, stilled!
Such mysteries, they yield all to one key
Had we the wit to know it, grace to use:
Life feeds on the living—all we know!
"In Him was life"—the sum of our knowledge, see;
No further oracle's vouchsafed to men
For all their restless searching, arrogant boasts:
That secret place where life doth hide itself

And thence flows forth to animate the worlds—
Rejecting Christ, THE LIFE, what hope have we
That any find it for us? Alternative,
There's none for us: 'tis Christ, or blank dismay!

As General spies weak point in his defence,
So Christ took His disciples, constraining them,
By force of that strong word they knew t'obey,
Despite their protestations—sure, not they
Would leave Him all alone to deal with this
Tumultuous multitude!—and, straight, they go,
Take boat as they are bid for further side;
And Christ, alone, took leave of all the folk,
Dispersed them to their homes, constrained by that
Authority in Him which some knew to name.

And was Christ alone? Two years had passed
Since in the wilderness one came and said,—
"The Kingdoms shall be thine and all their praise
Wilt thou but bow to me!" Two strenuous years
The Lord had carried water in a sieve,
Had urged great boulders up a mountainous slope;
The inconstant people slipped away from Him;
Fast as He raised them, fell to lower depth:
Is any toil like his whose high ideal
Urges incessant on unwilling souls?
What if, once more, the Tempter came and
      mocked;—
 "Two years gone by—no Kingdom yet to show!"
What if he urged, "Nay, try my readier plan,—

Let them make King of Thee, and all the gifts
Which Thou wouldst give to men shall flow from
    Thee!"
What if stress of temptation drove our Lord,
That He clomb up the mountain there to pray!—
And peace attends His prayer, and careful love.

The Lord gazed from His height; quick flash revealed
The Disciples toiling on uneasy sea—
Sight piteous out of the dark, their boat a toy,
A plaything of strong waves, tempestuous winds:
The men distressed with rowing make no way;
In the fourth watch of the night, there were they still!
"Anon, the Lord was with us, safe were we
'Mid all the turmoil of wild heavens, great seas!
Alone, we perish, late so full of hope!"
What greater strait might be—alone, in the night,
Peril of death about them, without hope?
But what is this adds horror to their dread—
Better to drown than demons see abroad
Walking the midnight sea! Spectre abhorred,
They'd heard how such appeared to men foredoomed,
And terror froze their hands to idle oars!

The *Shape* draws near—a likeness draws on them;
More awful fear appals: then,—Is it He,
The Spirit of their Master? He is dead,
And they, indeed, left orphaned, desolate!—
They cried aloud in terror; worse than all,
This apparition unendurable!

A tender voice bids all their fears subside—
They hear through the tempest's raging, "It is I;
Be of good cheer poor troubled hearts, nor fear!"
Too much the joy for Peter, sudden induced
On anguish of his terror:—Lost he his wits,
And cried, "Lord, bid me come if it be Thou!"
Hazards of faith are welcome to the Lord,
If it be so, He must reckless zeal instruct
Which counts not the cost. "Come," saith Christ,
                    And he came,
Stepped from the boat with eye fixed on the Lord,
And steady walked the waters: then, distract,
He saw the heaving sea; "I perish, Lord,
Save Thou!" Immediately the Lord stretched hand,
Took hold of the sinking saint, and spake reproof, _
"O thou of little faith, wherefor didst doubt?"
They in the boat knew their fears subside;
That dear familiar voice quick claimed their soul;—
How awful the surroundings, here was Christ,
And willingness took the place of shrinking dread:
Glad, they in the boat received Him; subsided straight
The fury of the storm: those weary leagues
Their sore-tired arms must row were over-past,
In the haven where they would be, were they now!
Once more they worshipped Him;—"By this we know
Of a truth, our Lord, Thou art the Son of God!"
The Lord, too, was He weary? What confidence,
The loaves, had they produced in hardened hearts
Which had no faith in Him when terror urged?

Walking on the Sea

Giotto di Bondone

VII
"The waves of this troublesome world"
(The Disciple)

THE WAVES of this troublesome world o'erwhelm us,
    too;
Our heavens are dark, and we are sore distressed;
We needs must right ourselves by our own might;
We bale out heavy seas with shallow scoop;
Exhausted arms still labour at the oars;
We scan the waters, not a craft in sight;
Alone, deserted, hopeless, dark, we wait
A greater wave to sink us! What worse case
Can happen to a man? But there is worse;
Till now we had judged things had gone contrary,
Misfortune'd overta'en us, unlucky fate;
Sudden, an awful Vision see we walk
Th' flood of our 'whelming troubles: all at once,
Aware are we; not flesh and blood we fight,
No, nor our fears or fancies; there is more;
Are powers of darkness leagued against us?
    Worse,
Doth an angry God oppose? Extreme our woe;
Welcome, rough billows of the stormy sea,

Or sudden sinking in its weltering flood!
Hair-raising apparition, who may face?
The worst has come upon us; now we know
What weapons God hath in His armoury!

In anguish of our terror, lo, a voice,
Pitiful, tender—sure, the voice of Christ,
Breaks through our abject dismay; speaks,—
   "It is I!"—
And, face to face with Him, we find our peace:
In all our misery, was He dealing with us,
In His love and in His pity, did He come?
Willing our hearts to receive Him in that bark,
The tattered, crazy vessel of our life:
He enters; now we know adversity
Hath but made opportunity for Him:
The troublesome ways of life are, sudden, smooth,
The far-off port as sudden is at hand,—
Christ in the vessel—all is well with us!

The bless'd mystery of the Church reveals itself
In glimpse we catch of myriad suffering souls
O'erwhelmed throughout the ages,—sudden eased,
Their troubles all assuaged in happy calm,
For that they hear,—"See, it is I, fear not!"
Good Lord, deliver us in all those times
When tribulation threatens to submerge!

"Ah, would I could believe this tale of peace!"
Saith one who has laboured for his soul's release

From all conditions asking faith and love:
" 'Tis impossible, that a living man should move
On the face of the waters:"
                  Impossible, indeed,
For any man to work this wonder: What,
If it were VERY GOD who walked the waves!

A little child spends half his happy days
In Faery; how else might he endure
The circumscribing of this straitened life?
We, too, are prisoned in a narrow cage;
"I can't get out!" we cry, to that free air
So proper for our breathing, to that large place
Where all is possible, and comes to pass!
No tribe of men so poor in fantasy,
But, lo, they make a way:—devils, or gods,
Shall know no let or hindrance! What if He,
Who knows what is in man, hath opened doors
By signs and wonders for our soul's escape,
And for her larger vision, that she see,
In common meat and drink and health and sleep,
Signs of God immanent? All things to Him
With whom we dare are possible!

VIII

Neighbour's talk

1st N. I tell you I was there and saw it all,
Ate of the bread and the fish, looked on His face
What time He raised His eyes and blessed the meat.
    2nd N. Was't good, that bread and fish, better
        than most?
    1st N. Why, no; 'twas common food like this we
        eat;
But when a man takes a morsel from God's hand
He thinks of the Lord, not of that bit or sup;—
Each morsel's wonderful, imparting life.
I scarce bethought me, erst, how God sustains
And gives their meat to men.
    2nd N. 'Tis so, no doubt;
Kidneys of wheat and beeves and fat of lambs,—
Think'st thou that these He might dispense as free
As yon scant barley bread and sun-dried fish?
    1st N. Hadst seen Him raise His eyes and give God
        thanks,
Thou'dst know that all the world's wealth is in His
        hand
To give or withhold.

2nd N. Why, haste thee, man,
Gather a multitude—Go, seek Him out!
Why languish we on scanty meat and poor
With a King and royal bounty at our door?
Feasts of fat things and wine on the lees are ours
So act we promptly.
   1st N.   Sooth, I know not, I,
If good things for their eating He'd bestow
On them who served Him. Not as liberal Lord
Of Feast upstood He there and dealt us bread:—
What matter bread and fish, so He be there,—
He, feast for famished mouths, anhungered souls!
   2nd N. Thou'st set thy heart on a man, like silly
       maid!
Haste thee, help raise a crowd and seek Him out;
Dream thou of Him; we'll see tables spread
With fat of the land in all the country-side!

❧

Lo, on the morrow, multitudes come forth
To seek the Lord who fed them. No boat was there
But that which brought the disciples; sure, must He
Be still where spread He table of the Lord
For thousands in the waste: impatient, hot,
They go round the water's head, or snatch at boats,
And find themselves where yestre'en they were fed:—
But they saw not Christ; only the trampled grass
Bore testimony; so took they boats and came
Back to Capernaum, aflame with zeal.

IX

"After the Lord had given thanks"

No work hath he whom the Lord loved to spare
For wonder of desert feeding, when Christ took
The handful of poor meat, and with one look,
One word of thanks to God, made ample fare
For all the multitude there:
What skill had the Evangelist to perceive
The meaning of the miracle,—to leave
All marvelling, and note Christ's thanking prayer!

Behold, the Eagle of the Faith fixed eye
Undazzled on the point of blinding light
Where Son and Father met,—that instant high
When men might *see* the Powers of Heaven unite!
For what great end? To give poor folks their bread:—
God makes it His concern that men be fed.

X

The sign and the loaves

*"Verily, verily, I say unto you, Ye seek me, not because
ye saw signs, but because ye ate of the loaves, and were
filled."*

Hot-foot, they find the Master: eager, cry,
And petulant as to favourite of the hour,—
"Master, when cam'st Thou hither? How hast come
With never boat to bring Thee? We have sought
There, where Thou fed'st us yesterday, in vain."

And Christ made answer, not to spoken word
But straight to the thought that worked, though
    scarce perceived,
Their act of seeking Him: full well He knew
That they'd been seeking; now, He tells them why—
(Ah me, how hidden things of the heart, unmeet,
Show up 'neath searching of Thy luminous Word!)
"Ye seek Me, not because ye saw the signs,
But because ye ate of the loaves."
            O Lord, why not?
Be there two sorts of men that seek Thy face

They who see signs and they who seek their meat
From God as the wild asses? Which be we?
To Him who hath comforted us and satisfied
We needs must cry to-day that we be fed;
Nor stop to ask,—What means it, then, this peace
Bearing us as a river;—all this love,
Food for heart hunger; this beauty spread abroad,
Bread for those famished who'd have all things fair;
This fulness spread for mouths and minds of men?
We take and feed, nor cry we on our God
Till some smart lack send us whining to His feet!
We see no signs, not we, we only eat
And whimper when a hunger falls on us!
Nay, children are we,—must needs cry on Him,—
"Our Father, give us day by day our bread!"
That crowd, nor we, have done so much amiss.

And, for they came to Him but to get loaves,
The just Lord holds them fit for better things,
Things ampler, fairer, than youth's fondest dream;
Content with that poor husk, the sign He gave,
Nor wanting more than more and better loaves,
Food of desire,—Christ feeds them otherwise
Than heart of man had imaged till that day!
Sage of the East, Philosopher of the West,
Keeps esoteric teaching for the few,
Disciples, chosen, who have followed him
Through teachings labyrinthine. Not so, Christ:
This multitude of ignorant, who came
For what He might give of tangible and gross—

He spread for them a table of the Lord
Their heart had not conceived of, nor eye seen!
But this supernal diet, could they eat?
Was that in them could deal with meat divine?
Yea, for Christ fed them free: nay, for some went,
Aye, many left Him, sick of heavenly food:—
His word once more divided men in twain,
Those who saw signs and those who sought the
    loaves—
Those left Him, those remained.

XI

The Divine offer

*"Work not for the meat which perisheth, but for the meat
  which abideth unto eternal life, which the Son of man
  shall give you; for him the Father, even God, hath
  sealed."*

Ye have come here for meat; ye hold that I
May serve you ever as I served you once:
For this, your thoughts have laboured:

Nay, labour not for meat which perisheth,
Which, having eaten, nought to you remains,
And soon again ye hunger.

For there is meat the Son of man shall give—
Which whoso eats is nourished all his days,
Nay, fed to life eternal.

This meat endures to everlasting life;
Sustains thro' every fainting and distress,
And never fails man's hunger.

"But what is life, then, Lord, and what is meat?
We thought we knew these two, if nought besides,
By many a sore endeavour."

Nay, there, my children, err ye; life is not
Getting and having fond things of the flesh,
Not these the things shall feed you.

See you, the Son holds life as one holds bread
And feeds the famished beggar at his gate;
So gives the Son to all men.

Who knows his life a gift, imparted straight
Moment by moment marked on dial plate,
Thinks not he can sustain it

By all his restless runnings to and fro,
By meat and drink his labours bring him in:—
These perish in the using.

But He who giveth life must needs support
With Bread He knows to minister at need,
Will men but come and take it.

For Him hath God the Father sealed for this;
For this, Anointed, that He might provide
Due bread to feed His people.

Behold the Son, sustainer of mankind!
For whatso dearth of body, heart, mind, soul,—
He holds the Sustenance fitting.

Let be, those labours that fail to nourish men;
Ho, ye that hunger, take the life I give,—
And daily bread to feed you!

XII
Good works

"What must we do, that we may work the works of God?"

Lo, there's a stirring and the dry bones live;
The breath comes into them, they utter words;—
"What must we do to work the works of God?"
So those Jews, and so we; sincere we cry,
When quicken'd of the Spirit:—"What must I do,
Say then, what must I do, to work His works
And please Him?" Much the living soul delights
To know there's a work for him to do,
Him, and no other. Doth he silent wait
Until the Lord make answer, show his work?
I trow, he answers as his will's inclined,
Nor knows he's his own oracle. He tries
This good work and the other; shares his bread
With hungry mouths, to sick folk ministers,
Leads the blind man, teaches the ignorant,—
To find that none lift voice to bless his steps:
"Ungrateful these poor wretched, dull the work!"—
So, wilful, leaves he that he wilful chose:

Then,—his home shall bless him for his kind good
   ways;
Is he not set to work the works of God?
But, slow, they understand not, those at home,
Nor choose their blessings at his hand to take:
Then "What's the good?" he cries; full sure, I've tried;
"The works of God, nay, they be not for me!"
Jesus answered;—hold still, good soul, and hear!_
Answered the word they spake, and the thought
   behind;
So ever deals the Lord with the sincere soul.

XIII

The work of God

"This is the work of God, that ye believe on him who he
hath sent."

"Nay, will ye understand, one work for you
Is set, takes all your days to carry through;
Ye ask of 'the works of God,'—there is but one,
Nor shall ye know when that is duly done:
(The little things ye do with mighty stir—
'Tis as if summer flies were buzzing there);
This, God's one work—believe ye on His Son—
Behold, the work shall please Him,—that alone!"

As shattering lightning struck that luminous work:
What then of all the teachings they had heard,—
"Do this and live?" What of that motion sure
In each man's breast bids him,—do well, endure?
"Nay, what is this 'believing'? Come we here
But to anoint Him King; we have no fear,
Not we, of Herod, Caesar, and their crew;
That thing the people willeth shall they do!

But we may die for this; what would He more?"
And, as they talked with hearts aggrieved and sore,
A shadow fell on th' palpitating crowd,
Awed them to sudden stillness: what hath cowed
These demagogues loud for their country's weal?
The Cross had cast a shadow each could feel
Lie cool, controlling, on his turbulent heart.
They thought upon the Lord:—He takes no part
Of all that wealth we covet at His hand;
We would be free; He goes as at command;
With feet fast held to the path He needs must tread,
He painful walks as one austerely led:
We, wilful, fain would rule with lordly sway,—
He,—"Father, do Thy will, I would obey."
We, all self-ordered, do the thing we choose,—
He, "sent," may no repellent task refuse.

And as they pondered, lo, the Cross grew plain;
Through sacrifice and service, grief and pain,
Men find the blessedness all would attain:—
Dim faith is dawning, they begin to see
The measure of Christ's word, "Believe on Me."
Lo, hot resentment stirs—in them and us;
"Unnatural," we cry, "that men should thus
Deny their instincts, dwell in painful strife
With all those things delectable in life!"

*"What doest thou for a sign, that we may see and
believe thee? what workest thou?"*

*"Our fathers ate manna in the wilderness; as it is
written, He gave them bread out of heaven to eat."*

They see Him as He is, and, sore at heart,
Fret and cry out against that better part
The Lord to each man offers. "What's the good?
Wilt thou provide us with sweet, ample food
Laid daily on our board? What sign dost Thou,
That, seeing, we shall Thy sov'reignty allow?
'Tis not enough all goodness to fulfil,
'Tis not enough to bend our stubborn will,
Till, seeing Thee, to goodness we incline;
Moses, before men's eyes, wrought greater sign,—
He gave them manna for their daily bread:
E'en so would we in idleness be fed;
Let's see and we'll believe; work sign to show
What great things Thou canst do; then will we go,—
But give us th' meat we crave,—Thee to proclaim
Our King—till all the nations own Thy name!

Lord, are we, then, like this insensate crew,
Insistent Thou their ignorant will should'st do?

XIV
The bread of God

*Verily, verily, I say unto you, It was not Moses that gave
you the bread out of heaven; but my Father giveth you the
true bread out of heaven.*

AH, Christ, Thy patience! Not wearied was the Lord
By the wilfulness of that so clamorous horde;
They, querulous, ask sign: lo, He reveals
The mystery, which stale use and wont conceals:—
"The poet, whence came he with burning thought?
The man, ingenious, who for his fellows wrought
New ways of pleasant living "the farmer, he,
Through labours manifold made bread to be?—
Not Moses or another gave you these:
My Father, that His children He might please,
Spread all this good before men day by day,
To nourish, comfort, gladden all their way.

"There be two signs by which ye shall discern
That Bread of God whose semblance ye must learn;—
All undefiled, it cometh from above;
It quickeneth men alike to life and love:

51

Ye see the signs; know what they signify;
All meat that nourisheth is from on high—
Whether that bread is secreted in small seed
Which sun and shower shall multiply at need
Of myriad hungry mouths, or spoken word
Quickening the fainting souls by whom 'tis heard:
Ye foolish ones, who deem your life your own,
Nor know that not all your labours can, alone,
Make food for flesh or for the spirit's need,—
Receive the bread I offer!"

"Lord, evermore give us this bread."

As sword goes through cuirass, conviction quick
Pierced the heart of the crowd; they knew them sick
For other bread than they wot of: "Lord," they cry,
"Evermore give us bread, or else we die."
They meant perchance no more than bread on board;
But not this niggard will the Lord accord
All living to His people:—our Lord, so we
Cry on Thee for our meat—our Sustenance be!

XV
Bread for all

"For the bread of God is that which cometh down out of heaven, and giveth life unto the world."

THERE is a bread of God come down
    From heaven unto men:
And whoso tastes that bread shall own
    Life, come again.
Thy pulse, is't sluggish, doth thy heart beat slow,
Doth eye lack lustre, feet refuse to go?
Poor famish'd soul, when fainting in the way,
Think'st thou Thy Father hath no bread to stay
    Thy sinking, then?

"My need is not as others';—love,
    My heart doth crave,
All ample meats and wealth above,
    My life to save!"
Your Father, knows He not? That bread He gives
Feeds with all fulness every soul that lives
And cries on Him for meat. Rejoice, sick heart,
Fulness of love, of loving, is the part
    Thy need shall have!

"But I—am weary of the dark,
  I fain would know;
  Would soar in heaven's high fields—a lark,
   My soul would go!
This little knowledge, sure, 's the spirit's curse;
Uttermost ignorance were hardly worse !"
Nay, fret not, soul; the knowledge thou dost crave,
All mind-contenting knowledge, thou shalt have—
  In unchecked flow.

"Well, for these others; I—want place:
  I would stand high!
  Would head my fellows in life's race,
   Pass all men by!
Will cities ten provide thee, eager soul,
Who know'st not yet; in My Name thou must rule
Ere thou be satisfied; must be content
To know thy ruling, serving,—office lent
  Thy Lord to magnify?

"As hart on water-brook I cry,
  My God, on Thee
O satisfy me or I die
  For want of Thee!
There is none other bread can ease my pain,
No other life is there can mine sustain;
Love, knowledge, power,—what are they lacking Thee?
O Lord, my Lord, thy servant's portion be,
  Come, feed Thou me!"

Lorenzo Monaco

The Last Supper

XVI

Manna in the wilderness

*"I am the bread of life; he that cometh to me shall not
  hunger."*

AN-HUNGERED in the waste Thy people go;
Scarce heard of men their feeble cry and low,—
"Our Father, give us bread! Remember'st not
How all that multitude rose up and got
The food they lacked spread there before their
    face,
And each one ate his fill, sustained of Thy grace!

"All holy, heavenly, undefiled, that bread
Came from above and Israel nourished:
Strong in that meat, they went alert and glad;
Filled with new life (late sore cast-down and sad),
The folk well-fed pursued their wilderness way:
Our Father, look on us who famished go to-day!

"We, too, in tedious wilderness tread slow,
Our brow is troubled, th' pulse of life beats low;
Aching for meat complain we bitterly,
Yet every need—a hunger known to Thee:
The time is come,—Our Father, hear our cry,
And feed with that sole Bread of God, can satisfy!

"Not Moses or another spread that board;
'My Father gave that bread,'—we have His word
Who came from heaven our Sustenance to be—
Sent forth of God for all men's misery:—
'I am that bread of God which they who eat
Shall never hunger more.'—Lord, feed us with this
    meat!"

XVII

The generous prince (The Disciple)

1

HAROUN AL RASCHID, mighty Prince,
Sought out a way should him convince
What every man in all the land
Would choose to have at Haroun's hand.
At nightfall,—when men were at ease,
And spake, each one, as him should please,—
Concealed, the Prince stood by and heard
His subject's self-revealing word.
The chase, the feast, the song, the dance,
All lent delights that should enhance
The prince's happiness each day:
But, wearied to satiety,
He sought out a new way of joy,
Should shield his people from annoy,
Should give his heart's desire to each—
That fruit hung most beyond his reach.

A wretched beggar woke one day
To find the prince at his door—"I pray,
Let me and all my goodly train

Eat meat with thee. Now entertain
Us royally as doth befit."
The beggar fell at the Caliph's feet—
"My lord, now what offense have I
Committed 'gainst thy Majesty
That thou shouldst bid me do this thing,—
Spread feast before my glorious King?
Nay, look, consider my estate,
These rags, this hut all desolate,
No crust for mine own hunger, I
Possess; sure, thou wouldst have me die!"
And wept the beggar, for he knew
His prince's anger would pursue
And slay him for some wrong he'd done.

"Nay, what a welcome, this, my son!
Rise up and bid us enter straight
To thy poor cabin desolate."
The beggar, trembling with dismay,
In fearful tones bade, "Enter, pray."
Haroun made straight for further wall,—
"What's this? Why dost not show me all?
Bring tools, strike down this wretched screen;
Nay, churl, let all thy wealth be seen!"
One blow brings down the flimsy thing;
A way is opened for the King.
But what is this? A palace fair
With costly furnishings is there.
Tables are spread with viands choice—
Rare wines that make man's heart rejoice:

To marble bath they lead the wretch,
Pour fragrant waters, towels fetch:
Lay clothing soft of silk and thread,
With costly unguents cheer his head:—
A new man, steps he forth to greet
His guests, in garb of honour meet.

Now, Haroun would his jest pursue;—
"Ha, ha! I have discovered you,—
Prince in disguise with palace grand
And five score slaves at your command,
And fountains cool and gardens fair,
An hundred precious things and rare!
This day we choose to be your guest,
Make haste and serve us of the best!"

That beggar, how shall he find word
To magnify his generous lord?

2

My King, and is it true Thy hands have made—
Unseen of any nor by sound betrayed,
So close it touches my poor house of clay
Yet shines not through the rents—a House which
    may
All duly entertain Thee, fair and large,
Fitted with beauteous furnishings—at Thy sole charge?

And hast thou spread a table to sustain,
Allay those hungers manifold that pain
Thy fainting mendicant? And is it near,
That feast prepared of Thee, doth not appear
For flimsy walls which close me round about?
My Lord, who spread'st the feast, make haste and let me
    out!

I, too, all washed and graced, would sit at meat
With Thee, my Lord, whose place is at Thy feet!
With morsels all delectable, appease
Those pangs ere now consumed me with unease:
But, what is this? The Bread I taste is—*Thee,*—
That manna duly fallen in the wilderness for me!

The wonder of 't! the while I idly thought
My hunger fed by any trifle bought
With laboured earnings, or bestowed of grace,—
Such simple matter little child might trace,—
A mystery's disclosed—my life is more
Than any meat men dress shall nourish or restore:

One only bread can feed me or delight,
Sustain for labour, fortify for fight:
My Lord, my Prince, and I, His beggar, see,
In bonds so close united are, we be
One flesh;—His very life He spends that I
May on His substance feed and live eternally!

The while I held my life a thing of nought
Fed on poor husks, mean things of man's contrivance
    wrought!

XVIII
Now (the Disciple)

THERE be, with lingering look cast back,
In Good Old Times see joy they lack:

There be who fix their wistful gaze
On what shall come with Future Days:

There be, acknowledge Now and Here
Their times fulfilled with liberal cheer:—

They hunger not nor even thirst
Who know in Christ their Last and First.

XIX
"Seeing is believing"

"But I said unto you, that ye have seen me, and yet
*   believe not."*

AND spake the Lord: "In this ye are condemned,
That seeing Me, yet have ye not believed!"

Ah Lord, those Jews, how happy, eye to eye
Might see the Son of Man in all His grace!
How could they not believe who Goodness saw
Incarnate in their midst! Sure, did we see
All love, all suffering, manifest in Him,
Then all the air were filled with beat of wings—
Our homing souls come fluttering to His breast!
How may a tale these ages past compel
As the vision of the Lord in our very midst!

Nay, pause my soul! The problem of our faith,
Lies it not just in this,—to see through a veil,
To discern the mystery of things unseen
Through common-seeming things of every day?
Perchance we easier the Christ may see
Stripped of poor trappings of mortality!

XX

Election

St. John vi. 37.

*"All that which the Father giveth me shall come unto me;
and him that cometh to me I will in no wise cast out."*

The Lord. ALL THAT THE FATHER GIVETH ME
    SHALL COME!
One of the crowd. Why, what strange doctrine's
    this? The Father gives,
Gives Him the souls of men, and lo, they come!
Another. Aye, but observe, He gives not every one;
God hath His favourites, and these, He gives:
I hate all partial ways; a father, here,
Fosters some sons, neglected leaves the rest—
Why, what a parent that, to choose 'mongst those
Whom equal nurture owes he, equal love!
And would ye say that God is such an one?
Another. Two parties be there to all contracts; see,
They whom the Father giveth, they shall come:
The choice is theirs, to come or not to come.
Would know that God has chosen thee? Go to Him,
The prophet,—so shall prove the choice of God:

Nay, 'tis a subtle net this Rabbi casts—
Who come to Him, why, they're the chosen of God;
Who, sportive, in the deep prefer their part,
Aliens are these.
    Another. But all sons may reject
Or take their father's counsel, favour, gifts;
This, no new thing; the VERY GOD must deal
With men as men shall will. Now, if I go,
Say to the Rabbi, "Master, I am come,
Do Thou Thy service of me"—who's to prove
"Tis not that God Himself hath drawn me thus?
But, hark, the Master's voice! He speaks again.—
    The Lord. AND HIM THAT COMES TO ME NE'ER CAST
       I OUT.
    The Last Speaker. Ah, that's the word for me! these
       many months
I've hung upon His lips, but dared not come,—
Say, "Lord, for Thy disciple take me now!"
For, see, I know mine own unstable mind,
How this day's choice, tomorrow I may hate;
And the behests He lays are very hard,
"Do this," flesh hates; "that," spirit shrinketh from:
But, if HE undertake, I may be bold;
If He will never cast me out nor let
My spirit fail Him, my proud flesh deny,
Lo, I will take that single service calls
My spirit to obedience,—I am His!

XXI

The chosen

"For I am come down from heaven, not to do mine own
will, but the will of him that sent me."
"And this is the will of him that sent me, that of all that
which he hath given me I should lose nothing, but
should raise it up at the last day."

"Why are your hearts sore for that word I said,—
Who come to Me believing, find fulfilled,
Yea, to the uttermost, all needs, desires,
Hungers and thirstings of their fainting soul?
Resent ye that a Man should undertake
All men to satisfy? But, see, I come,
A Servant, to fulfil My Father's will;
My Father, also yours. Can father see
His children lacking bread nor give to them?
So sent He Me from heaven to do His will
And give bread to His famished, ignorant:
As infants I must feed them! What say I
To Him that sent if one of these be lost?
Comes the last day, the Father looks for each
Of these His cherished children. It is His will

That who hath open eyes and sees the Son,"
 (The Glory of the Father, in poor weeds
Of this mortality), "sees and believes,
That man—he is alive for evermore
In fulness of glad living, joy fulfilled:
His mortal part, quick-buried out of sight,
That, too, shall live before God at the Last Day,
There is no dying for who knows the Son."

Our hearts aflame, we choose this better part;
We would believe and live, nor ever die!

In sooth, would we believe? Two several acts
Go to this consummation: we "behold"
The Son with steadfast gaze, adoring all
The beauty of holiness He manifests;
We scan the written page, and, one by one,
Figure the incidents that mark His days,
His healings, courtesies, rebukings, all
Those things He did, no man hath ever done;
Those things He told, no man hath ever known;
And, word by word, and phrase by phrase, we con
On our knees with tears and cryings all those words
Of awful moment spake He. *Behold* we thus
The Son, till the vision of His majesty obscure
All little majesties of earth; till Love, we see,
Infinite in tenderness and power to bless;
Till that strange wonder of the Godhead dawn
On eyes bedimmed—th' Humility of Christ:
"Behold" we yet, till th' awful vision rise—

The Cross on Calvary! We can no more,—
Our heart is broke with love and penitence.
Do we believe? We know that He is ALL;
That nought on earth desire we save Him,
And nought in heaven above. Lord, we believe:
We live, and nevermore shall taste of death
For He hath saved us; nothing loseth He
Of that made up our life; no tenderness,
No hope of better things, wistful desire
To serve our brother man; no joy in sound,
In sunset splendour, in a poet's thought;
No good thing of those things we name our life
Will He who bears us lose, as, quick, He lifts
Us into life eternal, where is God.

XXII
They murmur

"The Jews therefore murmured concerning him."

    First Speaker. "Come, I will give you sweets," the
        idle boy
Cries out, his idle comrades to annoy
When, empty-handed, find they him who cried!
Now, who is this, in our ears testified
"I am the bread come down from heaven for men,
And whoso eateth hungers not again"?
Sure, as an idle boy, He treasure cries;
You come to share and, lo, his treasure flies!
    Second. See you, He saith from Heaven He
        descends
To grace those men He numbers amongst His friends!
Why, on the face of it, this story's wrong:
Have we not known the family all along?
His father and mother, they live door by door
With mine in Nazareth: What would you more
To prove those words of His an idle dream
Of one who thinks things other than they seem?
    Third. Nay, hush, the Master speaks, and speaks to
        us;—
How hears He so far off?

XXIII

The invitation
St. John vi. 43—51.

*"I am the bread of life... This is the bread which cometh
down out of heaven, that a man may eat thereof, and
not die. I am the living bread which came down out of
heaven: if any man eat of this bread, he shall live for
ever: yea, and the bread which I shall give is my flesh,
for the life of the world. "*

THE LORD, a mortal Man, stood in that crowd
Of men so like Himself; He cried aloud:—
I am the living Bread, and who would be
Alive for evermore must eat of Me!

My flesh, the Bread that for the world I give;
And whoso eateth of My flesh shall live.
Your fathers ate of manna and they died;
Ye are an-hungered, lately satisfied;

But whoso eats the Bread from heaven descended,
His hungers, thirstings, pains of death, are ended:
Doth famine threaten—hastes he to the Board
Spread lavish for his eating by his Lord:

Not for the Jews alone, of chosen race,
Is there at My table laid a place:
Ho, ye that thirst, that hunger, come and eat!
The whole world would I at My supper seat.

But ah, not all will come to Me for food;
Not all know to discriminate their good!
There be, My Father whispers in the ear,—
These hear His word and haste them to appear:—

They sit and eat and rise up satisfied,
Happy of heart, of face beatified:
Believe, O men, there is enough for all;
Lend ear, ye careless, to the Father's call!

Would any father famish his own seed?
A father, knows he not his children's need?
My Father knows how, hungry, ye must go
Who seeks your sustenance in things below,—

For ye be more than these; ye may not live
On those poor empty husks the world can give:
These be of heavenly mysteries the sign,
But the food ye shall live by is divine.

Come, eat, My people, be ye satisfied;
Think on those victims that for Israel died;
Pictures are they, foretell how I should die,
A sacrifice for you to whom I cry:—
Come, take this Bread, My children,—it is I!

XXIV

A hard saying

First Speaker. A man like other men stands in our
    midst;
Cries, "I am bread, and ye must eat or die!
I am sole Sustenance of all the world!"
Mark you, not for the Jews he comes, the world
Shall share this sacrament, His flesh! All men
Shall come and eat—and there's to spare—His "flesh,"
As men eat sacrificial lamb. Nay, then,—
Perceives He fate we also see reserved
For the rash blasphemer?"
    Second. Know'st thou not His work,
How, doing good He ever goes about,
And where His feet have trod blessings arise
As flowers spring when an angel goes that way?
And, look you, I want more than bread to eat
Such as I bite and handle. Hunger have I,
Fainting of heart and sickening at my soul—
That no man ever offered to appease!
    Third. My spirit, too, has fainted; there was
    nought
In heaven above, on earth, could fill the void
That, gaping, ached in me. And then HE came;
His word filled all my hunger; He is bread:
I know it; I have eaten and am filled.

Fourth. These many months I've followed in His
     steps
As disciple; thought, poor fool, Messias come,
And looked to serve our King in some high place;—
My soul loathes this light bread of fantasy!
     Fifth. He offers us His flesh,—is there not tale
Of how the Baptist called Him 'Lamb of God,'—
As though the lambs slain since out of Egypt came we
Were shadows of this substance—cast before?
Sure, well enough we know that blood of lamb
Spilt at the altar cannot wash a soul—
Its flesh is body's food and can't feed soul:
What if He saith to us,—"Children of men,
Your least part is your body. Behold, there's meat
For those incessant gnawing hunger pains
That make a man faint at full board of this life!
There is one bread shall satisfy a man;—
Ho, all ye hungry, come! That bread AM I"?

And thus they strove, those Jews; conviction, straight
As well-aimed arrow, pierced the open breast;
The rest, infuriate with bitter scorn,
Beside themselves with rage that One should dare
Offer them sustenance as were He Prince,
In very deed their Lord—Giver of bread,
Cry out in wrath,—but can't escape His words:—
"How can this man give us his flesh to eat?"
Nor impotent their word; that selfsame cry
Hath bred division in the Church till now;
In these last days, perplex we yet with—"How?"

XXV

How can this man give us His flesh to eat?
(The Disciple)

WHAT legacy of discord have ye left
The Church of Christ, ye too contentious Jews!
The Lord doth offer Bread, and ye refuse!
Crabb'd contradiction hath your soul bereft
Of the sweet grace of God which bids men use
All common gifts of meat and light, nor lose
Least portion of His goodness while they ask—
"Nay, how can God fulfil so strange a task?"

His famished, fainting Church crawls on her way;—
"But how then shall He feed us? Is't in act
Of blessing? breaking? eating? that great fact
Of bread transformed to life He will display?"
An-hungered, we refuse our meat and say
"An knew I 'How' 'twere done, I would obey!"

XXVI
"How"—(The disciple)

THE children sit without the cottage door;
    Quiescent sit they—hands and feet at rest
And necks all stretched one way, where sits before
    Her little flock of nurslings, mother blest;
She holds full porringer and spoon, atilt,
    Her stool towards her children, brooding love
In all her posture shows; that none be spilt,
    Doth she with careful spoon lean from above
To where the three sit hungry at her feet;—
    Trustful, expectant, is the upturned face
Of every tender fledgeling, ah, so sweet!
    With ready mouths, quiet they sit in place
And wait unanxious on her ministering hand;
    Why should they fear? It is their mother feeds;
Wide-mouthed, they wait, nor eager make demand;—
    Their mother, knows she not her children's needs?

And every several mouth receives the spoon
    Until the bowl be emptied; satisfied
And glad the children play; but very soon,
    They'll come again for meat, and she'll provide;—

Feeding the Birds Jean François Millet

Again she'll sit with porringer and feed
 Her hungry brood; to-morrow, 'tis the same;
The children come with quick-recurring need
 For bread and love,—and doth their mother
  blame?

❦

Our Father, at Thy doorstep, see, we kneel,
 Wide-mouthed we wait the bit Thy hands shall
  give;
Thou who hast hungered, bring us now our meal,
That fed by Thee we may go forth and live
Strong in that meat which is Thy flesh indeed:
 We know not how Thou giv'st it; this we know—
As children nourished are we; utter need
 Supplied through all that Thou givest, strong we
  go.

Content Thy children go, and satisfied:
 With open mouth, we run to Thee again—
"Our Father, feed! that bread Thou did'st provide
 Is all consumed! This other time sustain!"
And He who loves us hastes to bring our meat;
 That meat which is His life He offereth free;
Grieves He that we should come about His feet,—
 His hungry children gather at His knee?

XXVII

(The disciple)

*"He that eateth my flesh and drinketh my blood abideth
in me, and I in him."*

How with Thou come, O Lord? I bend mine ear
To listen for Thy footfall drawing near;
And wilt Thou come and sit beside me here,
May I draw very close to Thee nor fear?

Beside Thee, with Thee, near Thee, O my Lord,
How good of so close place be assured!
More intimate and tender is Thy Word—
In Thee—the shelter Thou wouldst me afford!

Was never friend so intimately kind;
Scarce any lets me share his inmost mind;
A heart reserved in every man I find—
Thou hast, to take me into Thee, designed:

My soul, abashed, falls at the gracious feet
Of Him, my Lord, who holds me not unmeet,
All mean and sin-defiled, for place so sweet;
A closet in Christ's heart I dare entreat!

That other word to me Thou wilt fulfil—
To come to me; it is Thy lovely will
My heart to enter—keep within, until
All clean and gracious shows that domicile.

Lift up your heads, O Gates, the King shall come,
The King of Glory! He shall make His home
In this poor place of mine nor ever roam:
Who is the King of Glory? Let Him come!

XXVIII
The disloyal disciples

A MAN pours out his all—his love, his light,
His health or wealth it may be, all his ease,
At the shrine of one he loves; who looks askance,
Nor estimates his gift, but goes away
Half-insolent, half-careless, leaving all.
Rejected, smarting, cowers he in his place:—
What's left for him? Is't naught to recollect
The unsearchable riches by our Master spread
In that synagogue of Capernaum—all the good
A man might need—and they rejected all
Nor cared to know its worth? The Lord, He knows
The pain of the rejected.

    See them go,—
His cherished own disciples, who went with Him,
Sat at His feet and learned at His lips,—
With sullen shoulder, turn their back on Him,
And, dogged, choose their path, away from Him,
As though some wrong He had done them!
"Wrong enough,"
Say they, "to wreck men's lives on groundless hopes,

To offer them hard sayings of 'bread' and 'life,'
A bread man cannot eat, too hard a life,—
And this, in lieu of grace should come to them
In the royal court of their King!" "Why, who is this,
We've taken for Messias! All His boons
Are like fair clouds of sunset none may grasp!
How measure all this talk of 'flesh' and 'bread'
And 'life' and 'resurrection'! As a child
Who plays at armies, courts, and royal pomp,
The while there's nought to give or take away,
So hath He talked, and we, deluded, heard
And thought to prosper on those empty words!"
That synagogue—*Gethsemane found Him there.*

We grieve us at the hardness of men's hearts
Whose faith the Lord had built through many days,
Till now, they should perceive! Had we been there!
But ill-success, hard words, sore baffled hopes,—
Is our faith proof 'gainst these things? Have we left
Our all to follow Christ, and yet found nought,
Nor fails our faith at all? Ah, well with us,
Who come to feed on Him in days of dearth!
For, see you, Christ is King; one claim hath He—
The loyalty of subject-souls. Gem chaste,
Set in conspicuous place—man's loyalty;—
But there be foes the poor man would deprive
Of that, his ornament. How guards he it
From the base marauder? Well he knows the signs
That herald depredation; murmurings rise;
Nought is quite good enough for his deserts,—

Nor food, nor friend nor season,—no, not God!
Who murmurs is not loyal. 'Tis well we grieve
That Christ, aggrievated, cried to those murmuring
      men,—
"Doth this then make you stumble? What, and if
Ye saw the Christ ascend to God's right hand
To be there where He was ere time began?
I tell you, saw ye this supremest sight,
It were no more than words I speak to you,—
No more divine.

                "These things be real things,
Not dreams as ye suppose. Nought else is true.
But, say ye, 'Our concern is not with these;
We care not whether Thou be King of Heaven—
'Tis King on earth, who prospers, clothes and feeds
The men who serve him, we would have for Lord!'
I tell you, ye are wrong! The flesh ye serve,
Live to cherish with solicitous care,—
It profiteth not, that flesh, nor matters it
What ails it or what helps; of small account
Is the body and its clamorous needs before Him
Who is a Spirit. The Words I spake to you,
They too are spirit, life to quicken you,
Feed you with hope and joy and bread of love."

Ah me, that by the might of Him, our Lord,
We might perceive, if for a little while,
That our prosperings, failings, are of small account—
Touch not the life dealt out to us by Him

Who is our Life! Only a saint of God,
Like him of Assisi, doth rise at times
To show the worth of things, and which be life!

Christ looks on them—the false, the loyal souls,
And challenges the faithless:—"There be some
Of you, disciples, who have heard My words
These many days, have witnessed many signs,
And ye believe not yet!" Unmasked, they shrink
From His discerning eye; no more halt they
'Twixt two opinions; probation's past for these!
Disloyal souls, they go, to walk no more
With Him, their Master; reprobate, they turn.

And we, allowed to "walk with" Him betimes,
(As village lover *walks with chosen maid*),
Do we hold back and keep us in reserve
For higher bid of the world? Who nothing gives—
"Twould seem that the Christ of God cannot bestow
On that sordid soul and poor!

XXIX

"Faithful amongst the unfaithful found"

"AND would ye also go away?" Ah, Lord,
That anguish should compel so drear a word
From lips long-suffering! Forsaken, Thou,
As on the day when Calvary saw Thee—left!
Christ's human heart is wounded: who shall heal
Him who all healing holds for other's wounds?
But hark, one speaks; one of the Twelve stands forth
With healing word and mighty: not concern
For Christ dishonoured stirs his fervent speech:
A flash of the Spirit shows man's ultimate need;—
Shows him the one thing which that need supplies:
Go? Whither would they go when there's none besides
Him, their one Lord? All heaven is in His eye,
And what is there on earth to be compared?
Poor is He, bare of gifts, the proud man seeks?
There is one wealth alone shall satisfy;
He, Peter, knew; had tasted and was filled,
Believed that he might not for a single day
Forego and live. "Thou, Lord, hast words,
The Words of eternal life; these be our meat,
Without them there is nought to live upon;
Where go we then?"

Thrice blessed Apostle that thou speak'st those words!
All Christian souls rejoice and bless thy name
For that cup of cold water offered to our Lord
In this hour of His passion! Thou didst know
The profoundest mystery of our Faith profound;—
Some things there be of surpassing worth,
That, put in one scale and all the wealth of life
Heaped high in t'other, the high-laden scale
Flies up and kicks the beam, nor weighs at all
'Gainst that which holds—but WORDS—the words of
    life!
"Thou hast the WORDS of life,—to whom go we?
This things we have believed and surely know,—
That Thou art the HOLY ONE OF GOD."
              Relieved
From the intolerable shame of the Rejected,
We turn to see Christ eased and comforted;
But there be wounds which reach the seat of life
Not blessedest words can heal; the Lord replied—
No gracious words to Peter, His sure rock,—
"Have I not chosen you, the Twelve, and one,
Yea, one of you is a devil?" Deep the iron
Had entered into the Messiah's soul,
Our Lord, most pitiful! His human heart
Sunk 'neath those waves and billows God allowed
To overwhelm His Son; then, all the wrong,
The agony of Calvary fell on Him;
Nor might words solace in that darkest hour.

XXX

"And one of you is a devil"
(The disciple)

THAT man who entered hell and saw them there,
The devils, sinning with incessant stress,
Tasting no respite from hot wickedness,—
That man should know a devil, though he were
Grouped, one among the Blessed, taking share
Of all beatitudes that fall to these.
And we—what is a devil? We would know
The lineaments of fiends where'er they show.

Ah, well for us were all devils depute
To rage in hell-fire in some nether sphere:
What if the fiends we be should keep us mute
When words of love and trust should comrade cheer?
What if resentments raging without let
Should write us 'Devils" in their ceaseless fret?

BOOK II

Some Sayings of the Lord's

XXXI

The unwashen hands

"ALL seemly ways of life, how sweet they be!
How good to sit at meat from soil made free—
Due service order'd with the sedulous care
We give to prime occasions: we would share
Our bread with them who need, but there's a line
'Twixt us who eat prepared and those who dine
Straight from the market or the workshop come,—
With never rite of cleansing. Nay, our home
Demands this service of us; 'tis not pride,
Nor would we these, unwashed, with scorn deride.
But we may, hap, be separate; we whose plate,
Cup, cover, napkin, all,—immaculate."
(So mused a man whose ordered house was fair;
Nor knew he PRIDE sate Lord of all things there.)

Yet some disciples ate with unwashed hands,—
Performed not washings Jewish rite demands.

Ezekiel heard a whisper,—"Son of man
Sorrow shall compass thee, and thou must plan
To bear thy grief in ways men do not use;—

The desire of thine eyes at one stroke thou shalt lose;
Cry not aloud, nor mourn, nor shed salt tears;
Show thou amongst men as happy man appears,
Nor tell by covered lip nor any sign
That thou grievest under chastisement divine."
At evening his wife died: and in the morn,
He went as one who had no cause to mourn.
"Wilt thou not tell what meaneth it to us
That thou, a stricken man, behavest thus?"—
For Israel knew the prophet gave a sign
Whose meaning it behoved them to divine.

Those later Jews saw sign when Christ sat down,
And some of His followers made their freedom
    known
By eating, arrogant, with unwashed hands,—
As slighting openly the Law's demands.
The Pharisees spake, annoyed,—"What means this
    thing?
What doctrine alien wouldst before us bring?"
The Master's inner thought they had divined;
Now, how receive they His outspoken mind "

And the Lord spake:—

XXXII
"Corban"

"WHY vex ye a man with laws he cannot keep,
Cause strivings in his conscience,—which to do,—
Because of your tradition;—

Whether t' obey God's first law of love,—
Cherish his parents with his gifts and care,
Or bring gifts to the Temple?

'Corban' ye bid him call it, all that share
Of his wealth, his aged father's righteous due,
That ye lay greedy hands on;

He shall not honour father nor his mother,
That poor man; 'given to God' is all he hath,
According to your ruling:

Nor knows the man he gives to God then most
When most he honours them who gave him birth,
And keeps his God's commandment.

Ye hypocrites, full well Isaiah spake
Of men who should honour God with ready lips
While their hearts be far from Him!

Precepts of men ye teach as laws of God
(Rejecting all the laws which be divine)
For those do magnify you."

And, lo, the Lord turned from the Pharisees
And scribes, who offered there to hungry men
Dry sawdust of tradition:

And to the multitude of ignorant folk
He spake: "Now hear ye Me, and understand
Words that shall give you freedom!

All things that be without a man,—or meat,
Or drink, or cup defiled, or unwashed hands,—
In these is no defilement.

Not by what enters him is man defiled:
'Tis that proceeds from him makes him unclean,
Unmeet for God's high service.

If, greedy, he consume his meat nor think
To give to the hungry, if he drink in lust
Or craving for excitement;

If sloth constrain him all besmirched to go,
Unkempt, offensive to the eyes of men,
A shameful, slothful person,—

See you, 'tis sloth that makes the man unclean,
Sloth is his vile offence, not casual soil
Contracted in the market:

'Tis not his meat and drink that hurt the man,
But that consuming greed and drunkard's lust,
Come out of his heart, defile him. "

XXXIII

"Declare this parable"

HE left the multitudes and entered th' house;
The disciples, all-concerned, cried out on Him,
   "Lord,
Know'st Thou the Pharisees were wroth at words
Subversive of their teaching?" Said the Lord,—
"Fear not, My friends; though these be placed so
   high,—
Not placed of God are they; My heavenly Father
Hath not these rulers planted where they stand;
And every plant My Father hath not set,—
How high so'er it tower, how mighty wax,—
Shall sudden be uprooted, cast away.
Take, then, no heed to these imposing men,
Great in their own esteem. Blind guides be they:
If blind rulers lead blind people—what shall hap?
Lo, there be pitfalls ready to their feet!
Let them alone; behold, their day's at hand.

Then Peter, eager for all words of life,
Nor seeing yet that all the creed he knew,
Had sedulous learned from his infancy,

Pieter Bruegel the Elder

The Blind Leading the Blind

That Jewish ritual, tradition-built,
Crumbled to dust at breath of that single word!—
Said Peter, meek, but understanding not—
"Declare this parable to us Thy friends."

Ah me, the weariness and painfulness!
Did the Lord sigh, because that, day by day,
For many moons He had laboured to unfold
The secret of themselves to those dull wits:—
Would no words teach them, never sign convince,
What things were real, what were idle shows?
Nay, could they not perceive that, spirits, they
Conditioned were as spirits, with nought to hurt
But thought of evil intent; nought to bless
But goodness in a thought come home to them,
Or from them issuing? But pitiful
And patient always is the Christ of God:
Another time He laboureth to make plain
To these, His own, the rule shall try for them
Thenceforth their daily living.

XXXIV
Those things which defile

Nay, then, perceive ye not, e'en ye, My friends,
Why nought a man consumes defilement lends?
These things pass from him and their mischief ends:

Wherefore all meats are clean for whoso eats
Discerning,—cleanness cometh not of meats;
Nor washings, purgings, cleanse the soul of heats:

Are ye so blinded by mere touch and sight
That ye hold a man no more than in the light
Of common day appears to all men's sight?

I tell you, man is more than all those things
He takes and uses; from himself he brings
The worth he finds in these; he lavish flings

The glory of his praises on poor stuff
Not worthy nor unworthy, nor enough
To make his passing hours or smooth or rough:

Riches and poverty be lodged in him;
Nought from without his purity may dim;
From *him* comes all defilement—howe'er grim:

'Tis not the meat his mouth takes in defiles;
Out of him issues that his soul beguiles,
Odious uncleanness, soul-destroying wiles.

'Tis evil thoughts defile, not casual soil;
His evil is within him; all that moil
Of simmering ill-thoughts that in him boil;

All strife and bitterness, all wrath and hate,
The dull resentment that knows not to abate—
In a man's heart these, murders, propagate.

All lust, corrupting heart, destroying flesh,
Lasciviousness,—soul-enervating mesh,—
These things from man's heart issue, old yet fresh.

The eye which looks on other's wealth with spite,
The railing tongue which embitters all delight,
The furtive theft, contrived in dark of night,—

The arrogance, the folly, spoils a man;
All wickedness which mars the perfect plan
Of lovely living set for every man;—

'Tis these things from within a man defile:
There issues from him every evil wile
Which doth to wickedness his heart beguile.

"This, a hard word, O Lord! wherewith shall we
Cleanse th' poisoned spring that pure its waters be,
Draw love and sweetness from foul heart for Thee?"

XXXV
The woman who had faith

WE learn not her name or her lineage,—
   A mother, a widow or wife,—
One flash of the Spirit reveals her,
   Outstanding, as were she in life.
We know her as a Syro-Phoenician
   Acquaint with the life of the sea,
Familiar with th' ways of great cities
   Where merchants and sailor-men be:
Keen and subtle, she stands out before us,
   A Greek with th' Greek's ready wit,
Alert for the things which concern her—
   If aught her occasion might fit.

Poor mother, a sorrow consumed her;
   The sweet daughter she dearly loved
Was vexed with a spirit uncleanly
   That often the little one moved;
A neighbour one day came and told her,—
   "That prophet who teacheth the Jews
Hath left them and come to our border:"
   The mother's heart leaped at the news;

For many a story had reached her
    Of merciful deeds He had done;
How sued none in vain for His kindness,—
    This man—was He God's very Son?

So she came with her plea for His mercy
    (She knew how to name Him aright—
"O Lord, Son of David," she called Him),
    "Have mercy!" she cried in the might
Of a mother's petition, love-winged,
    "My daughter is grievously vexed,—
An evil o'erwhelms her—have pity!"
    He spake not: the woman, perplext,
Yet never disheartened, cried louder
    To Christ 'mid that group of His friends,—
Though cold and unheeding His aspect,
    And no one encouragement lends.

"Nay, send her away for she troubleth,
    Will soon raise a turbulent crowd;
The men of the city will chase us
    From thence if she cry thus aloud."
So spake the disciples, regarding
    Their Master, their safety, not her:
She heard; did her valiant heart fail her?
    The Master turns round 'midst the stir;—
His countenance shone on that woman
    Had come to Him full of her grief;
But the word that He spake was distressing—
    Gave never a hope of relief:

"Nay, thou art an alien, a Gentile,
  To the lost sheep of Israel come I:"
She would not take "No," but besought Him
  With ceaseless, importunate cry:
She fell at His feet and she worshipped,
  "Lord help me, for sore is my need!"
But He, "Nay, the children be hungry,
  I have Mine own people to feed;
Were it well to cast to the dogs, then,
  Their bread while the children go faint?"
Nor scorn nor indifference chilled her;
  She did but renew her complaint.

"As dogs then, my Master, regard us,
  Child and mother, unworthy Thy care,
But the very dogs under the table
  The crumbs are permitted to share!"
Now, lo, all the testing was finished
  The Master had brought to that ore,
The virginal faith of the woman,
  Ne'er tried in like furnace before.
Regard full of grace fell upon her,
  The Lord thought her worthy of praise:
"Great is thy faith, O thou woman,
  In gladness pursue thou thy ways:—

For, see'st thou, that word thou hast spoken
  Is balm to the wound of thy Lord:
What if I came hither from Sidon
  With purpose thy boon to afford?

What if I had watched thy young daughter,
    Afflicted, and seen thy heart bleed?
What if, for thy thoughts had pursued Me,
    I came to accomplish thy need?
No gift that a man hath to offer
    Is precious as faith in Mine eyes;
Go home then and find thy young daughter—
    Restored and in quiet she lies."

Saint Augustine in his Study

VITTORE CARPACCIO

XXXVI
Canis Domini (The disciple)

"THE dogs are fed:" Lord, e'en as these I'd be,
    But not alone for crumbs:
The happy dog doth still his master see,
    And at his call he comes.

So, blissful, would I raise dumb eyes of love,
    Would lie low at Christ's feet;
My Master's hand stretched to me from above—
    Were any joy so sweet?

And when my Master's chariot forth should go,
    Though inarticulate,
I'd run and tell the news to high and low,—
    That all might see His State.

He bids me gather in His wandering sheep?
    I'd race to furthest field,
And from all harm the silly wanderers keep,
    That I full tale might yield.

And when my restless ways disturbed my Lord
 He would but say, "Lie down;"—
A sudden stillness takes me at His word;
 My turbulence is gone.

Sometimes He gives me precious things to guard,
 A lamb, a little child;
Beside it, trusty, I'd keep steadfast ward—
 By bribes all unbeguiled.

And every day My Master's voice I'd hear
 Bidding me come or go;
And, looking up, would read in Countenance dear
 All such as I may know.

XXXVII
"He hath done all things well"

To that Decapolis He came again
Where He had left those hard, insensate men
Who bade Him quit their coasts for fear of loss:
Yet left He there a Witness to His Cross:

They brought Him quick a man afflicted sore,
Deaf was he with impediment; before,
These men thought only how to keep their wealth;
Now, pity bade them seek their brother's health.

Away from all the crowd He led the man;
A ritual of healing there began—
Whose meaning men might not as yet discern,—
Grown luminous for us prepared to learn.

All the sealed ears of men the wide world through
Impervious to His word, the Saviour knew
Present in this one man; each stammering tongue,
Which could not utter praise,—yea, all men hung,

Presented in that man, before His eyes:—
Is it for these, as looking up, He sighs,
The Lord is sad and wearied? Is it for these
He heals as in a parable,—who sees,

May know that touch of Christ alone can make
His stone-deaf ear to th' call divine awake;
May know, Christ's very Self must touch his tongue
Ere praise articulate by him be sung?

In the man's ears His fingers placed the Lord—
Ah, what a channel for the heavenly Word!
He spat and touched his tongue: did Christ impart
His very substance through this simple art?

"Ephphatha!" said the Lord, and at the word,
His ears were opened—happy man, he heard!
His tongue was loosened,—quick to utter praise
Of Him, restored him to men's natural ways.

Nor only the man praised Him, all the crowd,—
"He hath done all things well," they cry aloud,
"He makes the dumb to speak, the deaf to hear;"
Ah, Lord, our Healer, to our coasts draw near!

XXXVIII
The second feeding

Once more up slope of mountain climbed the Lord
With the propriety of him who walks on land
All in his fee. The swarming people watched—
That multitude from all the coasts about
Come to Decapolis to seek the Lord;
They brought the poor, sick souls belonged to them,
Their blind and lame and deaf, and many more
In whom the Perfect Image was eclipsed
By hideous havoc of disease.
Through many a weary march they dragged these
    sick,—
And here at last they found Him,—in wild parts
Of the eastern border, far from scribes and priests
Who hunted Him, the Just.
Now, toiling up the slopes they carried these
Poor helpless wretches to the feet of Christ,
And cast them there, to wait: He touched, He spake,
And, this one, that one, all, were sound and whole;
The friends who knew them saw the lame, go walk,
The sick, hale, rise up; ecstatic cried
The blind in joy of vision: the folk perceived

That from their God, sure, came this blessedness
And raised their hallelujahs.
                     Christ sat there,
High on the mountain where all might behold;
In slow clear words He taught the eager crowd,
With many pauses that they might receive,
As, careful, slow, one feeds a famished man;—
All day the Master dropped His sentences;
The night fell quick, and all the place was dark.

The Master held His teaching. Every man
From out his wallet drew light bed and lay
In slumber sealed: Ah, holy sleep, watched o'er
By Him, the outgoings of the morning made!
The early sun woke them from slumbers light;
Each ate crust of bread he had; and waited, then,
Expectant on the Lord: again, He spake;
All through that day the words of Life fell slow,
And every word some famished souls sustained;
In stillness hung they, breathing low for fear
A word should be lost; ah, poor for them the world,
E'en one word lost! All day they sat and heard:
Of judgment spake He? Of the Father's love?
Of place where every soul of man expands
To his perfection—the Kingdom of God on earth?

Spake He of healing, comforting and joy?
Of blessedness kept for the hungry soul,
The poor, the sorrowful, the lowly, meek?
Was none there, gathered up the words He spake,

Locked them in casket of his steadfast mind,
To be opened for our healing: as a man
Who beggar'd goes of wealth should have been his
Were but a will discovered, (surely made),
So we have lost those words, all due to us!

Again, night fell, and after scanty bread,
Again they spread their beds (who had them) there,
On such flat ledge on slope or at foot of height
As each could come upon; a city lay
Unsheltered 'neath the sky; nay, doubly safe,
All warm and cherished 'neath the love of Him
Watched o'er them from the mountain, tenderly
As praying mother guards her sleeping babe.

A third day passed as passed the other twain;
The Sacrament of Words sealed all their hearts;
And, as they heard, the vault of the blue heavens,
Each zephyr light that visited their cheek,
The swoop of wings above, wide stretch of earth,—
These sights and sounds so dear,—as organ tone
Accompanied His words and filled them out
With deep significance. Soul was alert,
Hungering the more for every morsel had,
But body, "Brother Body," fainting sunk:
Three days had they been there, and none was left
Of the scant meal they'd carried: home was far,
What help for them in this lone wilderness?

The Lord was very pitiful; He called
His Own about Him; gazing on the crowd,—
"I have compassion on the multitude;
Three days have they been with Me without food;
If I should send them hence, fainting they'll fall,
Unfriended, by the wayside." Those men of God
Remembered them of multitudes well fed
With store was meal for one man—two at most:
Did they bethink them, too, of mystic words
The Lord had taught them of the Bread of Life,—
Words had divided joints and marrow, caused
Zealous disciple to turn their back on Him,
And He was sorrowful;—what if it were,
That, as before those Mighty Words He fed
A multitude to show,—that all life was His,
That bread sustained men only as He bade;—
So now would He confirm that teaching hard,
A man's heart hovers round nor apprehends,
By feeding once again a multitude?
Such thoughts within them surging, those meek men
Yet asked,—"How feed men in the wilderness?"
The Master said,—"How many loaves have ye?"
"Seven." He bade the multitude sit down
There on the rocky, grassy mountain slope:
He took the loaves, gave thanks, and breaking them,
He gave to the disciples, they, to the crowd;
A few small fishes, too, He blessed and brake:
Thus, th' ritual was repeated—before and since
He taught that mystery of the Bread of God—
So that none could ponder but confirming signs,

JACOPO TINTORETTO

The Miracle of the Loaves and Fishes

That men indeed from God gat all their meat,
Should to remembrance leap, and none should doubt.
They ate their fill, that multitude of folk,
Four thousand men, with wives and little ones:
And the Lord sent them forth, glad, satisfied,
Great thoughts at work as leaven in their hearts.

Again, the disciples sent He forth to save
Of broken fragments, seven baskets full,
And as they went was this the hymn that rose
From hearts like springs whence issued thoughts of
	the Lord?—

<h1 style="text-align:center">XXXIX</h1>

Amen, Amen

THE mountains shall bring Peace—that mountainous
    land
    Where Bethlehem lies;
From out the little hills of Nazareth
    Shall Goodness rise
And flow among the people, a full stream
    In weary land;
The simple people sow and reap and eat
    On every hand;
Like rain fall'n on a fleece of wool He comes,
    Drops on the fields,
And lo, the barrenest patch the sun shines on
    Good harvest yields.
From sea to sea shall His dominion reach,
    And where He rules
The righteous flourish, put forth leaf and fruit,
    In the place of pools.
And favourable is He to the simple folk;
    The needy come;
The man who hath no helper makes his plea,
    And in his room

The Lord Himself makes answer; all the poor
     He shields and feeds;
And to their door, a river, copious, full,
     Beneficent leads.
The waters of that river, *Peace*, by name,
     Perpetual flow;
Nor drought afflicting other lands shall make
     This stream run low;
And in the valleys heaped, and on the hills,
     See, yellow corn;
His fruit shall shake like Libanus, and fill
     Wide Plenty's horn.
His Majesty shall bless the whole round world
     With mercies sure:
The Name of His Majesty, by the nations blessed,
     Shall aye endure.
          Amen, Amen.

BOOK III

The Transfiguration

XL

They ask for a sign

HE entered boat, and with His disciples came
To the western shore of fair Gennesaret:
Nor talked He with His friends, who, sorrowful,
Perceived that the cross lay heavy on their Lord:
As water poured through sieve seemed all His words,
And they, they nothing kept nor understood!
The people, too,—this present evil world,
Their thought and sole desire; nor knew they yet
That things they coveted nor got at all
Were precious only as they thought them so;—
They lent all worth to that which had no worth,
Nor saw the glory of the things they left!

The boat reached Magdala;—the scribes came forth,
And Pharisees whose spies had brought them word
That hither came He for whom hate laid wait,—
And quick they swarmed about Him, hating more
For that they heard was wrought in Gadara.
Guileful they questioned—would be shown a sign,
Comported them as eager for the truth—
The while they watched for single word or act
Which, before Sanhedrin brought, should justify
Them, murderous.

XLI

At sunset

As Christ and His twelve step from the boat, show
   they
Large, luminous, impressive 'gainst sombre skies,
As men in sunset glow take values on
And, monumental, stand. The heavens glowed,
Gennesaret shewed, a sea incarnadined,—
Half was red—as though some wounded god
(Hap, victim of Diana's certain aim)
Lay bleeding through the years till crimson flood
Spread wide as vault of heaven and reddened earth:—

Lo, here, a sign: did any save Messias
Perceive ensanguined sign of Christ, His blood,
Shed since the foundation of the world and now,
For the cleansing of the nations? With heavy sigh,
Outworn with weight of their infidelity,
He spake: "At even when the sky is red,
Fair weather, say ye, we shall have; at morn,
Ye see a red and low'ring sky; foul days,
Predict ye then with certainty. The skies,
Ye know how to read; learn the signs of the times:

Soon shall a blood-red sea wash the world's shores;
A night shall follow, black; and lo,—'tis fair:
The Sun of righteousness goes on His way
And all the world's illumined—but not you!
A dark and low'ring morn for you shall break,
Burnings and fuel of fire, and blood—not Mine
Shall quench the light of day. Why seek a sign?
The times be full of signs could ye but read."

Scarce finished had He these ominous words,
When sudden a dread vision rose before
The Saviour's presaging eye: against red sky,
(That sky of blood, Angelico, Brother Blessed,
With pigments fixed on consecrated wall)
Three lone shapes hang,—and One, the Son of Man!
Did the agony of those awful hours,
Of Buried nights and days, fall on His soul?—
"An evil generation and unclean
Seeks at My hand a sign; no sign is for them
But that of the prophet Jonah, for three days,
Entombed in a fish's belly."
                    He left them then,
Oppressed with weariness for the monstrous weight
Of the hard, obdurate hearts He came to lift:
And took they boat to go to th' other side.

How doth the city solitary sit,
So full of people once! A widow, she;
Once, great among the nations, now in thrall:
She weepeth in the night, her tears run free,

The ways of Zion mourn, her proud priests sigh,
Her virgins grieve, she lies in bitterness,—
City and people, they who asked a sign,
Nor knew to read that writing on their wall
Writ by the Son of Man who came to save!

Behold and see if there be any sorrow
Like unto My sorrow!

The Crucifixion

Fra Angelico

XLII

Of buying leaven

ALL men buy that which makes their bread to rise,
    Their daily bread;
Some leaven seek they, to make light those loaves
    Wherewith they're fed:
Take ye good heed what leaven ye employ,
    Lest it should be
That bread ye make distend a silly soul
    With vanity.

So, go ye not where Pharisees would sell
    Their leaven,—light;
Self-righteousness they mix in all bread made
    For their delight:
In holiness they think is theirs alone
    They walk the street,
Their robes held back, lest common men defile
    With touch unmeet.

See, too, ye go not to King Herod's men
    For that, shall make
Pleasant your bread of life and good for food:
    Ye shall not take
Least crumb of leaven that shall a man inflate,—
    Pleasure or pride;
Leave these to worldlings—better 'tis ye go,
    Unsatisfied.

XLIII
They fail to understand

Solicitous men buy that which makes their bread to
 rise,
For those small things they named
Their office, charge laid on them,—all the men,
Like fluttered doves, bethought them how they came
Aboard with but one loaf—how careless, they!
Well might the Master chide them! So, concerned
For their own petty failure, they let pass
Their Master's solemn warning, word of price.

The Saviour saw, and read the trivial thought,
Foolish self-blame, and pride impeccable,
Made turn deaf ear to Him, the faithful Twelve!—
"O ye of little faith, why all this talk,
This much-ado about so small a thing?
What matter if ye bring or leave our bread?
Know not ye that My words be more than bread,—
And, lo, ye let them pass, nor pause to think,—
What meaneth He? This leaven, what is it,
The Lord forbids us? Do ye not perceive?
Having eyes, see ye not? your ears, hear they,

128

And do ye not remember? That day I brake
Five loaves among five thousand, ye were there,—
How many baskets filled the broken meat?"
Afeared but not convicted, "Twelve," they say;
And wonder how that broken meat may serve
Present occasions—distributed long ago.
"And when the seven loaves I blessed and brake,
And ye dealt to four thousand, what took ye up?"
"Seven baskets filled we with the fragments, Lord."
Meek were they, but obtuse, for small affairs
Filled all their mind to its circumference,
Nor left them room for wonder: and the Lord's
    words—
Words pregnant with great meanings,—as idle song
Fell on dull ears too occupied to hear,
Or, hearing, comprehend.
              "Nay, have ye not
Yet understood that things be only signs
Whereby a man may interpret mysteries,—
The words of life I speak? Perceive ye not,
'Twas not of baken bread I bade beware?
Take heed of the leaven of the Sadducees,
Who scorn that word—'a man shall live by faith';
And, unbelieving, with light mind go forth
Denying, doubting, mocking at the truth
God's prophets witness for. Again, I say,
Beware of the leaven of the Pharisees,
Uplift with spiritual pride. No mocking scorn
Of humble faith is for you: not set for you,
The high seats of the mighty, complacent

In sense of greater goodness, purer faith,
Than others know; nor yet is't for you to sit

At ease where pleasure is the end of men:
These leavens be for others—but for you,—
Your bread, sincerity, no leaven lacks,
And truth is not puffed up!

At last knew they that He spake not of bread
But of the subversive teachings Israel got,
Poor Israel! of them at whose feet she sat;—
She, who misguided went, and fell in pit,
Discerned not of her, or of her blinder guides!
The Disciples bethought them of the leaven hid,
A little lump, in measures three of meal,
And, lo, that woman found her bread did rise!
With rising heart they conn'd the story o'er,
And knew the leaven in them—they went light.

XLIV

In the boat (The disciple)

Ah, Lord, and art Thou in our ship of life,
    That little boat!
And might we hear Thy words the while we row,
    Or lightly float?
But do we vex our heart with foolish cares,
    Lest bread should fail,
Or ever to the further coast we reach?
    Of what avail
Our silly fretting, that we had not thought
    Of all on board,
And brought with labour bread enough for all,
    A plenteous hoard,—
The while the Lord dispenseth Words of Life,
    Sustaining food
For all a man's occasions; living Bread,
    For all times good!
Be still my soul, nor vex thyself for naught;
    The Lord doth speak
Only to ear that silent knows to hear;
    To heart, made meek!

XLV

The blind man of Bethsaida

CHRIST and His following came to Bethsaida:
A man there was pitied of all the folk,
For he was blind; they led him to the Lord,—
Beseeching, Christ would give this blind man sight,
Make him as other men who go and come,
Joy in the sunshine, see the face of friend.

Ah, happy blind man! Jesus took his hand
And led him,—He, the Lord,—without the town,
Apart from all the folk: we are not told
Of beatitude that fell on that blind man,
His fingers held by Jesus: did he know
Of enveloping darkness more, or wish to see?
Christ spat and laid His hand on the poor eyes
All seared and painful: "Seest thou aught?"
    He said;
The man looked up; "Nay, surely, I see men!
As walking trees they're moving to and fro,
Ah, blessedness, to see men come and go!"
Again, the Master laid His tender hands;

EL GRECO

Christ Healing the Blind

Coolness and healing brought they; "Now, look up."
Steadfast he looked; to see mere bulk astir
Had gladdened the poor soul; but now, he saw;
The gracious lineaments of men were plain,
The little children danced, the women gazed,
Pitiful, glad, at him restored to sight;
The sun shone down upon them; trees were green:
The happy blind man saw, and saw aright!

The Lord gave sign which whoso will may read:
Behold, three stages in man's pilgrimage
Which every traveller treads:—first, we go dark,
And any leads who chooses to take hand;
Blind guides we follow tamely nor take heart
To ask, Where leads it, then, this path we tread?
Pitfalls full many lie in our way; sudden, see,
We sink, and find us bruised and hurt, we've fallen
In loathsome mire: then out once more we get,—
Scrambling, unseemly, all with mud encrust;—
Comes straight another ditch and in we fall!
One day, a Voice falls on our ear, a Hand
Whose touch is healing takes this hand of ours
And leads us on: a touch upon our eyes,
A softening touch as of tears and tenderness,—
We look up,—lo, we see! Alas, too long
Have sealed eyes blinded us to brother-men;
The world shut out, our sole concern, those things
That grieved, made glad, or fed, or sheltered us,—
Why, what were men to us? They passed us by;
Perceived we them in passing—solid things,

Which shut out the sun, obscured the light, what
    more?
But men like us, who gladness felt, annoy,
In sorrow heavy, or elate with joy,
Men whose concerns were nearer than our own,—
Nay, could we guess it when our eyes were dim?

Again, we know that Hand upon our eyes;
Is't doubt, or loss, or loneliness that lies
Athwart our failing vision? Sight is none,
Blackness of darkness gathers round our way,
The darker that we saw, if all amiss:
And, lo, the Hand, whose gentleness had touched
Our indurate heart, removes; again, we see;
And all men stand revealed: our *Brothers* go
Hasting in eager quest that way and this:
And we, solicitous, watch in dismay
Or glad congratulation; haste to help,
If but with fellowship of eye, the man,
Who endeavours for his kind: that other,—
    "Hold,
My Brother, see you, danger lies that way;
A foul infection's in the air; turn thou,
And walk where men go safe!"
            First, dark, we go,
In midnight blackness shrouded, nor see aught
But seek in the dark supplies for petty needs:
Then, vision comes, but dim; the men we see,
What wot we of their purpose? What to us,
The joys or pains another's breast disturb?

But there's a further stage; our eyes are ope'd,
And all men go, our BROTHERS! All that hurts,
And all that relieves poor men, 'tis ours to feel.
Enable us, Lord, that seeing, we go forth,
And, all the men we pass, for Brothers know!

XLVI

The journey northward

To Caesarea Philippi they walked,
The Lord and His disciples; the flowery ways
Of Galilee left behind, confronted them
The towering peaks austere of snowy Hermon:
The Lord was sorrowful; these difficult paths
Augured too well the way that lay before
His feet to traverse; nor, that wound, had it healed,
The disciples left who rent themselves from Him,
So tender to His own. Now, as they went,
He stepped aside and prayed—where else for Him
Was any healing found save in that fount
Eternal in the heavens, the Father's breast?

Did Christ the tale unfold of how, for those,
He had ministered and laboured, giving all,—
Wisdom and tenderness as daily bread
To them poor, feeble; of how the hour come
When He gave Himself to them, withholding nought,
Nay, offering of His flesh to satisfy,
And—they would none of Him! Prayed the Lord
   then,

For them who had not forsaken Him; that their faith
Should bear the strain of anguish He foreknew?
His countenance lightened, did the Lord return
To them who sate in awe—as men that mourn,
Called to a funeral, -aware of Grief,
His old acquaintance, sitting with their Lord?

"Who do men say that I, the Son of man,
Am?" asked He them: they paused to recollect
Various reports which had reached them.
"Some men say
That thou art John the Baptist come to life:
Others believe Elijah, sure, is come;
Was't not foretold? While other some perceive
That Thou goest sorrowful in the ways of men
And presage woes: but all men talk of Thee,
And some maintain that Thou that Prophet art
Whom Moses, having vision, promised men,
To give them laws and lead them." Unmoved, He
    heard;
And turning His godlike aspect full on them,—
"But who say ye that I am?" demanded He.

Ah, well for Simon Peter! Straight as clap
Of thunder follows lightning, out spake he—
Thank God, that there was one with utterance
    blest!—
"Thou art the Christ, Son of the Living God "!
Men have moved mountains, wrought stupendous
    works,

Have searched all depths, ascended awful heights,
Have loved, and given their bodies to be burned;—
But, see, the Christian soul who loves the Lord
Knows that the uttermost a man may do
In that hour was attained—when Peter spake!
Apostle, amply-graced, this second time
'Twas thine to say the absolute fit word!—
Was't not thy lips which spake -"Thou hast the
    Words
Of eternal life"?
        "Blessed art thou," saith Christ,
"Simon Bar-Jonah; not from lips of men
Hast learned this mystery which no man knows
Save as God tells him secretly: His hand
Hath lifted th' veil of flesh that clothes Me round
And shewn thy God to thee in the Son of man:
Peter, I named thee, and a *Rock* thou art,
For a man and his words are one, and thou hast said
Those words My Church shall rest on: I will raise
With myriad stones of grace a building vast
For the shelter of the nations; thou and thy words,—
That great Confession thou hast made this day,—
Shall, sure foundation, underlie the whole,
And, lo, the gates of hell, with hordes of fiends
Issuing therefrom all shouting blasphemy,
Shall not prevail to shake that Rock of Faith—
Assurance that I am the Christ, the Son of God.
The Keys of the Kingdom of Heaven I give to thee,—
For all thou makest sure with thine assurance,
Each soul thou giv'st to know the Christ of God,

Pietro Perugino

The Giving of the Keys to St. Peter

Into the Kingdom of heaven straight he goes,
And sings and sits at ease there: these be the free,
Whom thou hast loosed with thy great Word of
    truth,—
Thou, or another, holding this same faith.
But the words of truth he hears shall judge a man,
Shall loose him or shall bind: so thou shalt bind,
E'en by the words in which thou nam'st MY NAME,
The proud who will not hear thee, nor receive.
There is no liberty but in My Name;
And whoso doth refuse the Christ of God—
A captive goes he, bound with error's chain,
Oppressed and wounded sorely. Go ye then,
Loose all men in My Name, and lay those stones,
Each stone a faithful soul, which be My Church!
Nay, burn your hearts with the message, would ye
    haste
To proclaim this mighty Gospel, this Good News?
But ye shall wait awhile; tell no man yet
That He you follow is the Christ of God."

XLVII

The pilgrimage to Hermon

Now, see, exceeding sorrowful was the Lord;
And as they trod those stony paths, His word
Like molten drops fell on their shrinking ears;
    Their hearts were full of fears.

"The Passover draws nigh and we go up
That at Jerusalem I may drain the cup,
That bitter cup the Father offereth Me;
    And ye, My friends, shall see.

Your hearts are exalted, for ye heard one say,
'Thou art the Christ of God,' this very day;
And ye believe all power is in My hand,
    To do or to withstand.

My friends, ye have yet to learn, that to endure
More than a man can suffer is the sure
Infallible sign whereby the Christ is known:
    He suffereth alone:

142

Ye felt the smart, saw somewhat of the shame,
When false disciples did their Lord disclaim;—
Rejection is My portion; straight, we go
    Where no man will Me know.

The rulers of the Jews in council met,
Scribes and chief priests and elders, all shall set
Their faces as a flint; shall Me deny;
    Aye, they shall crucify.

But fear ye not; the Cross is not the end;
Though I be buried, yet shall I ascend:
On the third day God will raise up His own;
    I leave you not alone."

Thus sorrowful and very heavy spake
Our Lord who died for us: then one did take
The Christ to task that hard things He fortold;
    Peter, that follower bold,

With heart uplift for Christ had given him praise;
And he—trod gaily through triumphant days;
With Him to Lord in whose hand was all might,—
    Sure, every prospect bright!

So up he spake, and dared His Lord rebuke,
"Far from Thee, Lord, be this!" he cried and took
Hold of his Master's sleeve to urge his plea,—
    "This shall not be to Thee!"

His love insistent spake? Love comprehends;
Had Peter then no thought of personal ends
All frustrate should they bear this shameful thing—
        Rejection of their King?

Better to raise the multitudes, go forth—
New forces joining quick, east, south, and north;—
Who then would dare the King of the Jews reject,
        Or those His friends neglect?

Ah, Peter! erstwhile there was one who spake:—
"But worship me and I Thee King will make
Whom all shall haste to honour and obey."
        But Christ did say him nay.

So now He turned on Peter with rebuke
Severe as had the faithful saint forsook
The Lord he loved and served: "Get thee behind,
        I know thy worldly mind;

The things of men, riches and royal estate,
E'en these thy mind hath trafficked in of late
Since when thy faith I praised: Satan, thy name,—
        Woulds't woo thy Lord to shame?

For how shall I the work of God forget—
Disloyal as art thou? My Father set
This heavy rood before Me; shall I then
        Leave it for fear of men?

The things of God, the Kingdom and the Power,
Thou hast forgot in this the Tempter's hour:
To-day thy name is unstable Stumbling-block,
    Not now My steadfast Rock!"

And Peter—who may picture his dismay
As Christ's word penetrated him that day,
Revealing *in him* the ambition, lust of gold,
    For which his Lord was sold!

Good Lord forefend lest we Thy power would use
To further those vain ends we should refuse—
But thought we on the things our God doth will
    Our heedless hearts should fill!

XLVIII

The Cross imposed on all disciples

THE Lord turned Him about and saw them there,
The multitude that followed;—every man
Perfecting in his heart that crafty plan
Should profit him when Christ the crown should
    wear,
And hold the honours they all hoped to share.
But, hark, a word of searching 'mongst them ran,
Those eager men, each in his narrow span
Bent on self-serving: who for Christ had care?

"If any will in truth come after Me,
Companionless he comes; himself he leaves
Uncherished, all-denied, that he may be
My follower: he in his way perceives,
Asking his strength to lift, cross none may see
But who his daily ordering takes from Me."

XLIX

The Cross unperceived (The disciple)

But, Lord, my life is full of easy days,
The sun shines on me and my hours are fair;
If I be but a little sick, kind ways
Of household friends, solicitous, in care
Of me are spent: I never have a sadness
But Thou, my Lord, Thyself mak'st haste to cheer:
Yet th' shadow of the cross falls on my gladness—
Disturbs my soul with many a wistful fear:

For Thou hast bidd'n me, every morn I wake,
Go forth beneath my cross; that burden bear
Which my Lord carried also; but how take
A cross and bear it when none doth appear?
"My child, thy cross is ever in thy way—
That thing thou should'st—and *would'st not*—do each
    day.

L

Of saving our life and losing it

"THY life is precious to thee—would'st it save,
    Live in the light of the sun?
To that end great possessions would'st thou have,
    Would'st after riches run?
Nay, Child, thy life's first law thou fail'st to comprehend,
Nor see'st how th' life thou lov'st shall last until the end.

    Thou think'st to stay thy life with pride and praise,
        Fond braveries of the earth,
    Fat things and fragrant would'st have all thy days,
        Riches, renown and mirth?
Poor soul, a mystery be to thy fond eyes revealed—
Those choice things thou dost covet devour as a worm
    concealed.

    Nay, would'st thou save thy life? there is one way—
        A secret of great price—
    Pour out thy life in loving every day:
        Behold, the rare device
By which men give their all yet find the more to give;
The more themselves they impart, the fuller life they live.

    This life is good, thou say'st, there's nought beside;
        Let a man take his fill:

148

Bethink thee; all thy joy in life, thy pride,
    Come from thine own fond will:
What if these riches, joys, thou get'st with greedy haste,
Should of themselves destroy all savour of their taste?

That man lives and enjoys who hath a soul;
    But, if that be destroyed,
Not all the world shall profit him,—the whole,
    Into his net decoyed:—
Honours and wealth and power, all the fair things of life,
To him who hath lost his soul are weariness and strife.

But lose thy life for My sake every day,
    Nor seek thyself at all,—
Thou serv'st a Master who will surely pay;
    And to thy lot shall fall
To find the life thou losest; yea, of My joys to drink;
Through days uncareful, joyful, go—full glad to live and
    think.

But art ashamed of the Son of man,
    And of the words He spake?
The Son of God in glory thou shalt scan;
    For terror shalt thou shake,
And call on Him to save thee: to all, their deeds that day
The just Lord, He shall render; and from thee turn
    away."

Then spake the Lord to some disciples there:—
"Ye shall not die until Christ in glory shall appear."

LI

The Transfiguration (as remembered)

Months had gone by, and all those things were done
Which Christ should accomplish,—ere their fellows
  knew
Of that supernal Vision manifested
To three of their number—Peter, James, and John.
No matter how their hearts within them burned,
No word they spake, for Christ had bidden them,—
"Tell no man till the Son of Man be risen."

The Lord had been seen by several and by all;
At any turning they might meet with Him,
Their Risen Lord; at any instant, there,
In that same room, He might be in their midst:
Their hearts lay open as a viol tuned—
For Christ to play upon with word or sign,—
When the Twelve and their company assembled there,
In the Upper Room where Christ had met with them.
The Three held instant counsel; never, sure,
Would hearts be stronger, more alert to rise
To a great conception than were these the while
They waited lest, perchance, the Lord should come.

RAPHAEL

The Transfiguration

Then Peter rose and spake:—
    Peter. Bethink ye of that pilgrimage we made
Towards great Hermon, far into the north:
The Lord we know was exceeding sorrowful,
And told us plainly all which should come to pass
When presently we reached Jerusalem
To keep the Passover: And I, presumptuous,
I took it on me to chide my Lord, my God!
He called me "Satan," bade me get behind,
As one who ne'er had known the things of God:—
There be offenses tears will not wash out!
    John. Aye, but thou wast preferred before us all
Ere that dark hour: wert named the Rock, whereon
The Lord should raise His Church; forget not that,
In thy self-chiding.
    Peter. Christ bless thee for thy words
Of healing. But why hold your ears with tale
Already known? An eight days after that,
Christ took us three alone to the mountain's foot;
We climbed the slope;—ye know how the Lord was
    drawn
To mountain summits; how many times we've
    watched
And, tardy, followed upwards.—This difficult height,
Immense we scaled, till on a commanding peak,
The Lord knelt down and prayed. We too would
    pray;—
But, weariness o'ercoming, quick we slept;
We waked,—and lo, the Lord was there, but changed:
His countenance, glorious as the rising sun,

Compelled us to raise hand to shield our eyes:
The fashion of His aspect too was changed;
No more the meek Son of man He shewed, but KING,
Majestic in His lineaments; His eye,
Searching as light, outraying as sapphire cut
In hundred facets; an eye to see all flesh,
To pierce the secrets hidden in all hearts,
And spy out the hidden ways of all the world:
Wide, lofty, rose His brow, as it contained
All wisdom and all knowledge: justice and love
Sat throned on His lips, and all His mien
Acclaimed Him Sovereign Ruler of the worlds.
His raiment so familiar, that was changed
Was whiter than garment of any fuller washed,
Whiter than Hermon's snows that gleamed beyond;
Was glittering, glistening, dazzling to weak eyes
Of mortal man; ne'er from king's jewelled robe,—
His gold and purple thickly set with gems,—
Like splendour emanated. We beheld,
That day upon that mountain-ridge, our KING.
    John. Didst note the golden girdle girt His paps
As to confine the ocean of His love,
Richer than finest gold, that swelled within?
And sawest thou His hair, whiter than wool
Fresh from the combing,—whiter than the light?
Was't not the light of the Wisdom of God escaped
From trammels of the flesh? One other thing—
Saw'st how the dazzling splendour of His form
Cast rainbow hues on the mist, and lo, He sate
As on a rainbow throne, and, all about,

The rainbow-glory spread?
   Peter. E'en so it was:
(*And, turning to the rest*),—What John hath said
Doth put in words, he only knows to use,
Things all three saw but did not apprehend.
Lo, as the Christ sat throned majestical,
(So rude His throne!) on either hand, below,
Stood forms of stately men, effulgent forms;
As Lords in waiting on their King they stood.
They lifted eyes, and reverent spake with the Lord;
Some words we caught,—"Jerusalem," and "the
   Cross";
"The Law," said One, "this consummation shewed
Since first I bade men kill the paschal lamb
At God's command." We knew him by that word;—
Moses, the Lawgiver of our people, stood
Before our astonied eyes; the Second spake,—
"And all the prophets, following in my wake
Since the day the people cried,' The Lord, He is
   God,'—
Have carried on the tale, how Thou should'st come,
Be despised, rejected, betrayed to death, *for men.*"
Now knew we those two Great Ones; Moses, Elias,—
The Law and the Prophets,—come to serve the Lord
In th' hour of His anguish; upheld those two His
   hands
Even as the hands of Moses were upheld:
"It must needs be," their word, "else how should men

Be constrained to turn them round and seek their
    God?"—
"The Father watcheth, enduring all Thou bear'st,
The pains of the Son of His love; and all the hosts
Of heaven, wistful, desire they to look in."—

The glorious Twain spake, and were vanishing,
When upsprang my heart, as a man's who sees his all
Sink in the sea profound; I cried aloud,
If haply I might stay them: "Lord, bid us build
Three tabernacles here, for them and Thee,
So may we ever worship at the gates
Of heaven, ajar, far from the vexing world;
Ah, Rabbi, it is good for us to be here!"
So spake I, bold with terror, nor scarce knew
That I dared intrude on that High Solemnity.
Sudden, a cloud enwrapp'd us and the Three;
We entered the cloud unwilling, sore afraid,
Uncertain if 'twere death, or th' end of the world:
When, lo, an awful voice spake issuing thence,—
Distinct and final as no words of men—
"This is My Son beloved; hear Him, ye men,
For in Him alone of men I am well pleased. "

The blackness passed; silent, the Voice; the Men,
Glorious as seraphs, had vanished from our view:
The Lord stood there alone, His garb the same
Which He ever wore; but still His countenance shone
Radiant in splendour of that heavenly scene,
And we fell on our faces, sore afraid.

Then came the Lord and touched us with the touch
Of our familiar Friend, no longer strange,
And bade us rise and be no more afraid;
Immediate, looking around, none saw we there,
But Him and ourselves, and all was as before.

LII

The Three ponder

Now James took up the tale:—
   James. As we came down the mountain, spake the
      Lord—
Was there a new authority in His tones,
Or was't that we had seen our glorious KING,
And knew Him as He was?
           "See that ye tell
To none those things that ye have seen to-day,
(But take ye courage from them—ye, and I;
For heavy hours are at hand),—until that day
When the Son of Man shall have risen from the
   dead."
We asked each other then, but asked not Him,—
How may a man make question with his King?—
"What meaneth He by this rising from the dead?
When they shall kill Him, will He take up life
As that young man, that maiden, and go on?
And should He die, and die, an hundred times,
Yet will He take up life and walk the earth?"
A marvel, sure; but all men know the truth
When they find it; this, not the truth we sought.

Pondering in silence went we: many things
Perplexed our minds, made wondrous clear to think:
One said, "If Thou, the King, be come, why say
The scribes, our teachers, Elias must come first?"
He answered us:—
      "Elias cometh first, restoring all,
Turning to wisdom disobedient hearts,
Making the mountains low, the valleys high,
Restoring highway where a man shall walk
And praise the coming King. But what of this,—
The King that should come—He is the Son of man;
'Tis writ that He should be set at nought and sold,
And suffer many things. Have ye read thus?
Elias—he hath come, and none perceived;
And on him they have wrought their evil will,
E'en as 'tis writ. Prepare your hearts, My friends;
The Son of man shall suffer at their hands,
E'en as did he."
      Then all at once we knew,
He spake of John the Baptist who had died,
Slain for the truth.

LIII

Christ descends the mountain

Peter. Ye know the rest, for ye were there below,
What time we descended from that holy place
To a shelf of the mountain where were many folk
And where ye waited, wondering. Ye all know
How, seeing Christ still radiant, luminous
With some faint show of the glory we had seen,
The people were amazed and ran, saluting,
As saw they Caesar standing in their midst—
Nay, the Messias of our expectation!

One poor man separated him from the throng
And came and knelt, telling a piteous tale:—
"Lord, I beseech Thee look upon my son!
Have mercy on him, he is my only child,
And a dumb, deaf spirit hath him in possession:
When all goes well with the boy, this demon comes—
(We know it's there by the poor boy's sudden cry)—
And straight it dasheth him down and teareth him,
And after it hath left him bruised and sore,
My poor son pineth."

(How well we know the signs
The wretched father tells to Him should cure!
But not so sure are we that ills which destroy
The flesh and wear the spirit come from source
Malign, opposed to God and His dear grace.
We, confident and sure of our place in the world,
Are sufficient of ourselves for our ills and good—
What need for gods or devils? Ah, who knows!)

More the man said:—"I brought him to Thy friends,
And prayed their help; they could not cure my son."
And Jesus, still ashine with the light of heaven,
Spake kingly: "O faithless people and perverse,
How long shall I yet be with you? How long bear?
Bring hither thy son to Me." They brought the boy,
And as he came another dreadful fit
Seized the poor child; he foamed and wallowed there;
The pitying crowd looked on; the father wept;
"How long," saith Christ, "hath th' boy been in this
        case?"
"From a child, and oft the demon taketh him,
As one in savage wrath, and casts with force
Demoniacal into the fire, or Sea
As to make an end on him: and, watched I not
Incessant, long ago had the child died
At hand of th' awful enemy we see not."
The man took breath,—to see in the face of Christ
The dawn of his hope. "But if Thou canst do aught,
I beseech Thee, have compassion, help us twain!"
And Jesus, pitiful, said, "'If thou canst!'

Not thus shalt thou command the help of God:
Thy power it is that is lacking, not the power
Of Him at whose feet thou kneel'st: go, get thee
     strength,
For the hardest, happiest task falls to a man;
Believe, and all is possible; thy prayer
Is answered ere 'tis uttered; all might's lent
To him who can believe; see, he commands
The power of God to his bidding!" The poor man
O'erwhelmed, amazed, by the blinding light
Of so great revelation, cried straightway,
"Lord, I believe!"—and even while he spake,
A crowd of doubts came knocking at his heart,—
Who then was this Man, claimed the power of God,
Nay, placed that power, almighty, at the hest
Of any beggar crying "I believe"?—
But struggling with the demon of his doubt,
Lo, faith was born in the man; he lifted eyes,
Saw the compassion of the Christ, and cried,
"Help Thou mine unbelief!" Ah, happy man,
To him was discovered th' secret of all strength!
And of his gains he gives us: now we know
That any poor wretch crying upon God,—
Believing that God hears him and will aid,—
Why, that poor soul goes strong in the strength of
     God
And knows—*all's* possible—whate'er his need:
Nay, should his need be that, unable, he,
To be sure of his God, even for that there's help—
"Help Thou mine unbelief!" his cry forlorn,—

And faith steals in, soft as the silent dew
That comes no man sees how to bathe the fields,
And lo, the fainting blossoms quick revive,
And every slender blade upholds itself!
Thus was't with the man,—he knew his help had
    come.

Then Christ spake direct word to the unclean—
The dumb deaf spirit which had seized the boy—
"Come out of him, I bid, nor enter more."
We others,—sore possessed with anxious fears
Or jealousy, or lust of forbidden things,
Or base suspicion, envy, hate or greed—
Whate'er it be, our torment, seldom quit,
Or quitting, but to come again more fierce—
We wait, breath held, to see if Christ indeed
Was strong to expel the fiend that poor boy took
For his very self!—If we too might have hope!
"Come out of him,"—saith Christ; but not at once
Will he relinquish that convenient place,
Once more will he have free play; with awful force
He tears the anguished child;—compelled, comes out,
But leaves the boy as dead. We know the way
Of this kind; have we not cried on God, and help
Has come, but the last conflict—ah, how sore!
The crowd who had come running up to see
Cried, "He is dead,"—and in their hearts accused
The Lord who had healed of having slain the boy:
But Jesus took him by the hand, and raised,
And gave him to his father; the boy was cured.

"Pooh," cries th' sceptic, "what evidence bring you
That aught had happened but the fit was past
And the patient enjoyed a respite?" Wiser men
In th' wisdom of this world would have gathered
    proofs,
But these, who spake the thing they knew, bring
    none.
In every crowd are witnesses who swear
That this thing they saw done; more testify
With adjurations that it ne'er took place—
Be the thing so usual as were fainting maid
Carried out of th' crowd. How vain is testimony!
And men who know the word they speak is true
Go not about to prove their spoken word,
Assured that he who hears may test the truth
By inner witness to its verity.

The majesty of God filled all the place
Where Christ had wrought this wonder; there was
    nought
To see but hushed crowd—the boy restored;
But yet—there was the majesty of God!
And each man worshipped there as he knew how.

The mountain left, the Lord and the Twelve sought
    house
To be removed from the people for a space:
As children shamed, the nine, perplexed and sad,
Besought the Master:—"Tell us why we failed?"

Forbearing, gentle, Jesus told them why:
"'Twas not for lack of power—that were as nought:
No man is censured that he fail to use
Power which he lacks: but having power to help,
And withholding that same power from one who
    needs,
The man offends both God and his brother man."
"But, Lord, we lacked the power, we tried and failed!"
"Nay, then, ye know not yet wherein consists
A man's sole power, without which he is nought;
With which, he is almighty to command,—
For see, he wields the power of the Almighty.
Because of your little faith ye failed to-day:
A little have ye, scarce enough for this,—
This kind's exorcised only by strong prayer;
And men pray not to God with sincere mind
Except they believe that He is and that He hears
And grants their prayer however great it be,
E'en wer't to plant yon mountain in the sea!
A grain of faith small as a mustard-seed
Hath strength enough to move earth's solid base
But ye-how little faith is in your hearts!"
"Lord, we believe-help Thou our unbelief!"

LIV

Of opposing mountains (The disciple)

AH, Lord, we see great work which calls on us—
Work that should ease some pains of suffering men,
Make some crushed brother lift his head again:—
But who are we to make a mighty fuss?

Some better man perchance is summoned thus—
Monition secret comes and he'll be bold,
Nor care tho' men should shew indifferent, cold;
As mountain-mass obstructive, they, and callous.

This task is not for us: it is too hard!
"And know ye why?" saith Christ; "your little faith
It is that hindereth you from great reward:

Believe in God, nor shrink from any scathe,
Nor fear the frowns of men; it shall be done—
What thing thy Father bids believing son!"

LV

"They were exceeding sorry"

THEY left that region desolate, and came,
By devious ways and sweet through Galilee;
A green and golden sea stirred by the breeze
Was all that prairie-plain of ripening corn;
Peace was abroad in all the yellowing fields;
Velvet anemones and the lily tribe
Left no place bare for treading; pigeons wheeled;
Great seas of corn and barley, fields of flowers,
The humming of innumerable bees,
High in the heavens, a lark—pure song, no more—
These be the things that make Galilee a dream
That a man remembers while his right hand keeps
Its skill. The villages lay, dull red, blue,
With flowers and women on their garden-roofs;
The village elders,—grouped about some door,
Clad each in long red robe, blue-edged, and wrapped
With sheltering folds round head,—discussed at large
All that had come and gone that day, news brought
By hot-foot messengers these fifty miles:—
Sweet Galilee, beloved of the Lord!

Not now would He make known His presence there,
But enters village where men knew Him not:
While all men marvelled at the tales they heard
Of words He spake and wonders He had done,
None guessing He was there in their very midst—
While thus men talked and dreamed,—Christ laid a
     task,
A heavy labour on His tenderness:
Who hath not had, sad messenger of grief,
A letter, urging -"It gently break to them,"—
The well-beloved, of husband, father, sick
Unto death, nor like to mend? Who hath not shrunk
From grievous part of breaking loving hearts
With news of anguish? Did the Christ feel less,
Did He love less, or less was He aware
Of the orphan'd loneliness for them He should leave?
So while the people talked and dreamed of a King,
And royal pageantry was in the air
For all the excited folk of Galilee,
A sorrowful company kept themselves from men:
The Lord taught His disciples; said to them,—
"I have a thing to say of grievous weight;

Give heed, My friends, let sink into your ears,
Nor be distract by the hopes of the multitude:
We journey to Jerusalem, and ye think
The hour is come when th' KING shall be
     proclaimed:—
I tell you, nay; to the hands of wicked men
The Son of man shall be delivered up;

And they shall kill Him; there is no reprieve:
Hope not 'gainst hope that Jehovah, sure, will work
A great deliverance—triumph o'er His foes:
Deliverance shall come,—but after death:
Three days shall the Son of man lie, being dead,
And after three days He shall rise again."

The men were exceeding sorry; that was all;
The Master's sorrow overwhelmed their hearts,
And they sat amazed with grief; but not a word
Of all that Christ had taught with heavy pains
Did these men understand; their minds were veil'd;
Sorrow of Death and joy of th' Resurrection
Alike were hid from them; nor dared one to say
To their Lord, "What meanest Thou by these dread
    words?"
Who hath not hid him from the physician's doom
That all he loves, his dearer life, condemns?

LVI

"Lest we cause them to stumble"

SILENT and sorrowful the Company went,
Pondering the Master's word with sinking hearts
And tardy comprehension. Once again,
Their steps turned to Capernaum, the blessed,
And the Lord made His abode in Peter's house,
High honoured to receive Him; where was she
Late raised by Christ, His grace, from fevered bed,
Who fain would speak her love in household cares:
Did the Lord find comfort there in the sorrowing
   Twelve,
Or sat they there with Him, as those men of old
Sate silent with stricken Job?

          Peter went forth
And was accosted by those men sent out
To gather from Israelites that Temple due
The legal half a shekel. "Doth not your Lord
Contribute to the general fund?" they ask,
Surmising that, perchance, for cause unknown
He might refuse this service to religion.
"He doth," said Peter, knowing well his Lord

Neglected no observance that became
A pious Jew. But th' Saint went home perplexed,—
Now where should he a shekel find? Full well
He knew that Christ no money owned—though He,
The Son of God most high! Entering the house
With anxious brow, the Lord discerns his care,—
Speaks first to him, or e'er he told a word:—
"What think'st thou, Simon, of whom do kings take
　　toll,
From their own sons, or from the subject-folk,
The strangers, not their kin, o'er whom they rule?"
"Why sure, from strangers." "Therefore," saith the
　　Lord,
"The King's own sons go free and share that State
The tributes of the people must support."

Did Peter understand how the Lord had said,—
These Temple-dues are for God's worship paid,
That th' beauty of holiness may be set forth
By outward symbols in the Temple: See,
I and the Father are one; that worship paid
By pious souls to God, is paid to Me—
One with the Father, sharing all His dues:
Is't fit that I contribute toward those rites
Ye Jews pay punctual to God—and Me?

"But we may not impede these men in their task,
Nor give them cause for anger or harsh words,
Misjudging thee and Me: so their offence
Were laid at our door who had made them sin:—
Go thou to Gennesareth and cast a hook;
Draw the first fish to land, nor pause to ask
Is't small or great; when thou hast ope'd his mouth,
A shekel thou shalt find; that take and pay
To the men—just Temple-dues for thee and Me."

BOOK IV

Of Little Children

LVII

Of greatness

When all were in the house, the Lord looked
    round;—
"What matter, then,discussed ye by the way?"
Not one would speak; shamefast, they held their
    peace;
Knowing that He knew their thoughts, how say to
    Him
That, as they came, lust to be first moved each,—
First in the Kingdom, the King's high Vizier,
The Lord of all the people under him!
They played for a high stake, these humble men,
And, hap, because their hearts were sore distress'd
Comfort they sought in visions of high state
And wealth, more than these Roman rulers knew!
That this dream should come to pass not one had
    doubt;
But a perplexity remained,—whose claims
Would the Lord recognise when He was King?
And each one showed Christ had conferr'd on him
Some singular honour, set him above the rest;
But none could assure his heart that he was first;

Then anger rose, and each made haste to blame
The presumption of his fellows, yet none saw
In himself—the offender who had most presumed.
Nor yet had wrath died down, though shame was
    come:

Now, tender as a mother, sat the Lord
And called His Twelve about Him. Knowing all—
Their pride, presumption, bitterness of soul,
Their chiefest sin, that they had Him forgot,
Yea, when He spake of anguish close at hand,
And thought of their own advancement;—never word
Of harsh reproach hath He, of wounded love:
From tangle of thoughts unlovingly, chooseth He
What of lawful, lovely, He might yet educe,
Nor shame the men He loved with open blame:—

"To be first among his fellows—who shall chide
The man who hath generous ardour to be great
Knowing that greatness is for service lent?
Promotion cometh not from North or West,
Nor comes by favour, nor for goodly parts:
See ye, My friends, this hope is for you all
And I will show you how ye may attain
The first place in My Kingdom: Who would be first,
He must be last of all and serve the rest,—
A slave to fetch and carry and be chid,—
Nor ever fret him; this, for the love he bears
To the men he serves for my sake and for theirs."

The Disciples heard, amazed; and, subject long
To the arrogance of scribes and priests, and lords
Set over them by Rome,—sustained by hope
That they in turn should lord it arrogant
When Christ should come to His Kingdom—half in
    wrath
And half astonished, sore for th' words they heard,
The Twelve who knew none had such claims as they
Indignant cried,—"Who shall be greatest, then,
In th' Kingdom of Heaven?"
              Christ called a little child
(Was't Peter's boy, at play about the house?),
And with fond hand He set him by His side
In the very midst of th' Twelve; regarded him
With tenderness divine, and said to them,—
"Think not of place in the Kingdom first or last:
Not yours to enter in except ye turn,
Quit pride and envy, love of place and power,
And be as little children, simple folk
Who're not concerned for vain things of the world;
Humble yourselves as these, and ye shall come
To the Blessedness where is no first or last."

LVIII

"Of such is the Kingdom" (The disciple)

In the Kingdom art the children;
    You may read it in their eyes;
All the freedom of the Kingdom
    In their careless humour lies.

Very winsome are the children,—
    Say, whence comes it, their sweet grace?
Small the pains they take for goodness,
    Scarcely know they Duty's face.

Frail and faulty little lieges,—
    Yet well-pleasing to their King:
Scanty thought they take to serve Him;
    Yet the chosen Offering bring;

Ours, the weary long endeavour;
    Theirs, the happy entering in:
Ours, to strive and wait and labour;
    Theirs, to joy before the King!

"Except ye be as the children,
   Have ye in my courts no place:"—
Lord, how meekly would we ponder
   The glad secret of their grace!

Not in holy painful living;
   Not in tears nor suppliant prayers;
Not in white days free from sinning,—
   Not such sanctity is theirs.

What do they to take the Kingdom?
   Only this leave they undone—
Suffering Christ the King within them,—
   They in nought invade His throne:

On the children's brows no witness
   That themselves do fill their thought;
In the children's hearts no strivings
   That to them be honour brought.

Therefore finds the King an entrance;
   Freely goes He out and in;
Sheds the gladness of His presence;
   Doth for babes great victories win!

LIX

"Little children abide in Him" (The disciple)

"I write unto you, little children, because ye have known the
Father."
"I write unto you, little children, because your sins are for—
given you for His name's sake."
"And now, little children, abide in Him."

YE children, unto you I write:
    Not strong to overcome are ye,
    Faithful to strive nor wise to flee:—
But your weak coming was in Light!
    Ye see; though not your feeble thought
    Can shape the knowledge Light has brought,
Yet have ye known the Father long from wisdom hid.

An older breast with pity swells
    For babe in this rude world bereft
    Of parent love, all des'late left!
Uncareful and at ease he dwells;
    He knows, yet knows not that he knows,
    A care that bears him as he goes,—
The Father he discerns and smiles all fears amid!

And, children, unto you I write!
    Ah, not the shining of this face
    Nor shelt'ring of the Father's grace
Has kept your garments wholly white:
    Poor babes, ye sin-for strong is ill,
    And small your might and weak your will—
Lo, swift forgiveness lifts anew to His embrace!

For not on you the burden lies:
    A gracious cloud, a tender tear,
    Is all ye know of hireling fear;
Then into joy again do rise:
    E'en while ye sin, are ye forgiven
    For His Name's sake: wherefore in heaven
Your angels evermore behold your Father's face.

For, ah, wise little ones, ye know
    To take the Off'ring at the door,
    Nor question aught nor tell the score,
But enter, free as winds that blow!
    Wherefore, O little ones, I write
    That ye do keep you in the light—
For loving must ye be, O children of His grace!

LX

The greatest in the Kingdom

"Came the disciples unto Jesus, saying, Who is the greatest in
the kingdom of Heaven?"
"And Jesus called a little child unto Him, and set him in the
midst of them."

WEIGH his estate and thine: accustom'd, he,
To all sweet courtly usage that obtains
Where dwells the King. How, with thy utmost pains,
Canst thou produce what shall full worthy be?

One "greatest in the kingdom" is with thee,
Who all-unhindered sees the Father's face,
And thence replenished glows with constant grace:
Take fearful heed lest he despiséd be!

Order thy goings softly, as before
A Prince; nor let thee out unmannerly
In thy rude moods and irritable: more,
Beware lest round him wind of words rave free:

Refrain thee; see thy speech be sweet and rare;
Thy ways, considered, and thine aspect, fair.

LXI

The child's humility

"Can any humble him as this little child,
Nor think of himself, but of this beauteous world,
Of all those things God made to pleasure men,
Of the fair folk, each busy in his way,
Of Him who made the world, and loves all men?—
Who thinks on these things, not upon himself,
Whether he's first or last, or good or ill,—
That man is first in the Kingdom, for he knows
To take as a simple child what God provides,
Nor frets him whether he be first or last."

And, as He spake, the mighty love of God
Embraced the child; He took him in His arms
(E'en at His side the child was too far off!),
And all that love wherein His worlds subsist
Went out to little children!

"Behold, the little children are with you!
The innocent little ones who make no claims
Nor seek themselves at all! Consider them,
The little children, how they grow, nor ask,—

'What shall we eat or drink, or how be clothed?'
But rest them happy in their Father's hand,
Nor cry nor strive for wealth or place or power;
The world and heaven are theirs—what is there more?
The glorious sun careering in his might,
Casting his jewelled splendours on the earth,
Cold, colourless, without him; all the stars,
The wonders of the heavens; the butterflies,
The little birds that sing and glance as gems,—
These are the child's; the beauteous boys and girls
To whom fond arms he stretches, all th' fair men,
Women who stop to bless him with their smiles,—
Mother and father, sister, brother dear,—
Those wondrous things to know, and these, to love,
And all, to bear him as on mother's lap;—
And all the loving, his own Father's love,
And all the treasures, his own Father's wealth,—
That princely child, aware, goes forth in joy
Of that high estate which none may take from him.

"A king sends out with royal state those men,
Ambassadors, whose part it is to show
The King's high will and manifest his power:
And, who will not receive the lords he sends,
Those men are his enemies and feel his wrath:
Thus come the children, graced with heavenly gifts,
Discovering the Kingdom by their ways
And by that wealth of blessedness is theirs:
Receive them in My Name; and, understand,
The children slighted, I am slighted too:

But one such little one whom ye receive
With reverent joy as coming from the King
To manifest His pleasure,—in that child,
Me, ye receive; lo, I am with you then;
And whoso Me receiveth, the Father, straight,
Takes up His abode with him. 'How is't,' ye say,
'That the Great God can come by th' narrow way
A little child shall open?' Learn ye first
That the least among you is the great one here;
Then shall ye comprehend how God doth come
To every heart that opens to a child!
Humble yourselves, My friends, so shall ye know."

LXII
Humility (The disciple)

How deep a mystery, my Lord, Thou shew'st!
   Though I do beat my breast and humble me
And of most servile tasks do make my boast,
   Yet have I not attained humility!

Then, more I shame me, think upon my sins,
   Cry, "Lord, I am not fit to touch Thy feet!"—
My self-abasing no advancement wins,
   The more I loathe me, more am I unmeet!

"Perceiv'st thou not, my child, what thing I ask—
   The lowly, simple grace that children own;
Thy Pride imposeth every heavy task;—
   Humility is one as Christ is One:

Fret not thyself, but set thine heart on Me,—
And thou goest garbed in My Humility."

LXIII

The wonder of innocence (The disciple)

INNOCENCE has no problem
For him who thinks his soul a castle, fed
From without at his will; a keep whence he may bring
Evil or good, as disciplined hath been
His will by life's affairs; and where he is
Alone with himself, impregnable: as he,
Nor helped, not let, doth make or mar himself,
So is he innocent, unmade, unmarr'd
Ere habit of false thinking or ill deed
Has fitted to his shape.
                But the poor man,
The hunted soul who has no innermost
Where sin is not at home, who strives t' escape,
Who hates and yet inclines, and, desperate,
Cleaveth to Grace to save him from the Thing—
Is it himself?-that daunts him; who finds not where
T' abide; but when, of tears and cryings brought
Into the place of peace where is the King,
He, thinking to remain, doth let him out
To dwell at ease, sudden, he findeth him
In outer darkness, under other rule;—

Then painful, winneth yet again to where
He was before, but not to abide; for aye
Filling laborious a vessel bottomless!—
This poor man holds the Innocence that shines
In the face of a little child a mystery,
The deepest and most precious God doth keep.

LXIV
The Fall (The disciple)

ALAS, sweet souls, ye fell! But no so low,
Ah, not so low as we! Abashed are ye
Where God was all a separate self to see;
And, naked, conscious souls, ingenuous go

To hide yourselves for shame! Your Fall's worse woe—
Th' inevitable "I"-inherit we:
Our child-souls quit their paradise to be
First in a fall'n state that day they know

Themselves for entities, with passions, parts:
Alack, the difference! Ye who did dwell
In th' light of God see from what height ye fell,
And shun the recreant Self that filch'd your hearts:

No gracious shame's in us; complacent thought,
Approving or contemning, 's Ego fraught!

LXV

Offences of pride

THE Twelve fixed eyes upon the child in their midst,
And pondered the Master's words: "Here's a new
   thing,"
Said each in his heart, "This teaching, who can hear?"
And each intolerant thought, impatient word,
All hot resentment and all hasty scorn
Stood manifest in light: the little child
Sits not in the seat of the scorner, is not wroth;
And, who were they that they should set them up
As more than other men, with the right to judge?
The child's humility as leaven spread,
And humble for the instant stood they there
Before the Lord who is lowly.
             Then spake John
(Knowing he answered straight the word of Christ),
"Master, we saw one casting devils out
And using Thy name to bid them; we forbade;
He is not of our company,—by what right
Used he Thy name of power?"—thus questioned
   John;
Arraigned for arrogance, he sought excuse:

But Jesus said unto him,—"Forbid him not;
Who made thee that man's judge, or how shalt plumb
The depths of faith hidden in any heart?
'He followeth not with us,' say ye in your pride;
Think ye God hath none other way for men
To tread but that ye follow? Humble you;—
So shall ye see God deals in many ways
With the hearts of men; and he that's least of you,
Nay, he that is outside, may do great works;
Sure, such an one will no light evil word
Speak of Me, in whose Name he acts. Say ye,
'He hath no knowledge, Lord, of all those words
Thou taught'st us from the beginning!'—what know
    ye?
God is not shut in by any bounds men draw,
And say, This way or that the Spirit goeth:
Let this rule guide your thoughts:—that man's for us
Who sets not his face against us: all the good
That any man may do, he doth for God,
Tho' strangely he misname the Lord he serves.
But should one know My Name and for My Sake
Do any deed of service for My friends—
Cup of cold water given to one of you
Because ye are Christ's—I say to you, in truth,
That man shall have reward at the hand of God,
And shall in no wise lose it.
                   But, if reward
Wait him who serves, though small his service be,
Likewise believe ye that no slight offence
Escapes its condemnation. See this child—

These little ones believe as a man draws breath;
E'en as the unreasoning babe its mother trusts,
Unknowing of trust or love but in the act,
So do these little ones believe in Me
Though My Name to say they know not. See to it
That ye cause them not to stumble: each offence
Of arrogance or violence done to these,
All careless living they're to follow fain,
All light regard of God they learn of a man,
These things shall as a millstone hang on his life:
Nay, well for that man were a millstone hung
about his neck and he were sunk in the sea!

LXVI
Counsel (The disciple)

As they are wariest guides who most have met
Mischance themselves, thy mother's slips may yet
Shew thy feet, daughter, places to eschew.

As, sweet the mother-walk, but perilous!
And flowers do cheer the progress hazardous,
Tho' heedless pilgrims chance on bitter rue!

But thou, my daughter, meekly glad, hast ta'en
A man from th' Lord; thy joy hath wholesome pain
Of diffidence, safety's sole pledge, for here,
Danger avoids, assurance keeps, in fear!

So hold thy soul 'neath heaven, as April earth,
Waiting the fall of counsel; nor in vain;—
Who hath so graced thee to a blessèd birth,
Will not his wisdom's waterings refrain.

LXVII

Of offences against children (The disciple)

RECALL, when soul of Law convinced did rise
For baby-trespass to thy startled sight;
How, shamed, the wee transgressor sunk his eyes
Knowing beyond thy knowledge of the right,
And meek 'neath thy chastisment. Keep him now
Under the Law as then; that, as he grows,
"Due followeth deed in course,"—the rule he knows
His times t' interpret. and, Law-compell'd, be thou,

Nor drop some heedless trespass in his way,
That, stumbling over, his weak knees shall fail.
Offence shall come! but do not thou betray
His soul to sin. Yet, oh, without the pale
Of love's sweet use, no banishment accord
For any sake—lest thou malign they Lord!

LXVIII

Of occasions to fall

A GRIEVOUS vision saw the Son of man:
His tender plants, the Twelve, and all who hung
Insatiate on His word, saw He beset
With occasions manifold to make them fall;
Their path must they pursue as men who tread
'Twixt points of spears uplifted; no escape
Was possible for them; it must needs be
That th' occasions come which make a man to fall;
But, "Woe to the world that scattereth
    stumbling—blocks,"
And, "Woe to the man through whom the occasion
    comes,
For the fall of one of these, My little ones,
Become as children in simplicity!

But, ah, My children, many things without
Shall be as offences fallen in your way
Which your feet shall scarce avoid; the lusty world
Compels you in his pride; insidious friends
Woo to disaster which they name your gain,
And spread those tempting things that work your fall:

A man may save himself from all offence
Which he keeps without him;—but how hard his case
When his own heart and hand, his eye and desire,
Stretch out in longing for the forbidden fruit,—
So good to feed those raging hungers there,
In a man's secret heart! so apt withal
To make him wise with the wisdom of the world!
'Who shall forbid,' say ye, 'what a man desires
And may take at his will to please himself?'
He shall forbid himself; shall see the fruit
Fair, luscious, of desire, nor stretch out hand,
But be as maim'd, his reaching hand cut off!
Nor lets himself perceive the tempting thing
Dangled before his eyes; an eye plucked out
Were as open to images: nor shall he go
There, where the wicked sitteth to entice;
Unable he to run in the ways of sin
As man with foot cut off who halting goes:
Better to enter as one halt, blind, maimed,
Into th' Kingdom, than hurry with both feet
To where the fire of lust goeth never out;
Or with eyes covet, greedy hands snatch, fruit,
That burns who eats with thirst unquenchable!"

LXIX

"Everyone shall be salted with fire"

Fret not, My children, for so hard a lot:
Would ye keep fresh in the rank, pestilent world,
That flaunts it bravely, banners all unfurled?

Would ye escape the noisome crew that in hot,
Unwholesome places are in swarms begot
And cloud the air, or lurk as maggots curled
Within a man to corrupt him—till he's hurled
To th' foul Gehenna where unclean things rot?
Would ye, I say, go clean? Then must ye be
Salted with fire: temptations must assail,
And ye must fight to victory, or flee
Before the attack is made: ye may not fail
Or go, a captive wretch, dishonouring Me,—
As though the power of God might not avail!

LXX
Of salt and humility

Have salt within you, friends,—the truth of God
Which sweetens and keeps sweet the flesh of men;
But, hark ye, salt may lose its proper savour:
Beware, lest so ye bandy words of Mine
In common speech, each man to prove his point,
That, though the word be true, it has ceased to mean
Or good or evil for the man who speaks!
Ye shall not speak or think the words of life
But with due reverence; with soul convinced—
Heart, mind, and tongue-that by these very words
The man who hears shall live: nor think to pass
That salt to others is as dust in your mouth:
Have salt, I say, in yourselves; and should the Truth
Be to your taste stale, flat, and profitless,—
Have salt, I say, again: God shall replenish,
Add truth to truth till ye shall live thereby:
But offer no man as his salt of life
Truth that hath lost its savour in your mouth:
How season salt that hath its saltness lost?

'Whereby,' say ye, 'shall we know if we have salt?'
The man whose life lacks savour fretful grows,
Sees hindrances in comrades of the way,
This man and that annoys him, trespasses;
Then is he angry, chides, says scornful words
His fellow resents; and, sore, they take their way,
Still side by side, with enmity at heart!
What ails the poor man, miserable, that he
Goes vexed and vexing neighbour, that he breaks
That vessel delicate—a household's peace?
The truth hath lost its savour on his tongue;
Forgets he his poor part and the grace benign
That takes him, a worm and no man, and exalts
Till, as one sees far set on a mountain's crest,
So he discerns—the lineaments of God!
Thought he on these things, how should he resent
The little slights, offences, that befall?
Would ye be certain that ye keep the salt
Which shall preserve you to eternal life?
Ask,—"Do I dwell at peace with every man,
For God is good, and I—of small account,
And,—is there a man who is not more than I?"

LXXI

Of despising children

"TAKE heed that ye despise not one of these!
Behold, I shew you a mystery; children come,
Not all divorced and separate from Him,
Their Eternal Father; not given o'er to men
To use as shall please them, cherish or neglect;
Continual commerce holds the Father still
With His children, lent to men; for every child
Hath his angel who beholds the Father's face,
Bears quick report of all the little one's state
And carries instant back the Father's love
To wrap the child, invuln'rable, from the world,—
Shield from the rubbing harshness of men's use
As invisible mantle,—down of mother bird;
Then, how despise ye them God cherisheth?'

The Disciples heard; with eyes ope'd wide in awe
They gazed on th' child in their midst as they had
    seen,
Sudden, a glorious angel standing there,
Still shining radiant from the face of God:

FOLLOWER OF REMBRANDT
Manoahs Sacrifice
"How shall we order the Child"

Then, gathering courage, spake they:—"Lord, make plain
   plain
To us, how we despise thy little ones
Nor know our offence at all? Sure, we, Thy Jews,
Have ever cherished offspring—brought them up
In the fear of God, abiding in the Law,
And precious to us as the gift of God?
Remember we how Eli spoiled his sons,
How Solomon bade use the rod betimes,
How Manoah and his wife the angel prayed,
'How shall we order the child?' E'en so do we,
Our nation by its families, importune!"

"Aye, cherish ye the children, as one holds
His own possessions precious,—kine in field
Or jewel in its casket,—so the child!
Said I not to you,—Ye shall not despise
Or think to possess a child, who yet is God's—
The while he sheds his radiance in your ways?
Which then is more-a man or his possessions,
E'en the costliest he hath? So ye're assured
That each of you is greater than a child;
That what ye give must needs be his increase;
That what ye say with wisdom edifies!
And so the child,-one greatest in the Kingdom,
Graced with nobility in heavenly courts,—
Is taught to frame his life on mean exemplar,
To covet baubles, think your shallow thoughts!
Ye deem the child has nought but what ye give,
Ye, or the ancestors ye reckon yours;

That while he's little, he may scarce do well,—
'Wait till he's grown'-become as good as a man!
So, lax, ye rule him, 'What knows he of law,
A silly child, unknowing right or wrong!'
Despise ye so the children, nor perceive
That God hath writ on th' heart of every child,—
'Obey, and thou shalt live; transgress, and die:'
The infant child still sucking at the breast
Knows this thing,-till ye teach him to despise,
As ye yourselves despise, the Law of God:—
Idle, ye bid him do some idle task
Nor heed when 'tis not performed. The child comes,
   meek,
Beholding you as gods to whom right and wrong
Are as ye choose to name them. Quick he learns
To do as ye do, transgress as ye allow,
And day by day forsakes him that fine sense
Whereby discerning good and evil came he.
Thus, ye despise the children.

Ye think, ye wise ones, ye alone can know
If ye be learned, all the ways of God,
If ye be crafty, all the hearts of men:
'The little child, great thoughts are not for him'—
So think ye in your arrogance, and provide
Baubles and petty trinkets to amuse
Him whom his Father thought on from the first,
And planned a playground filled with various joys—
Where little feet may wander, hands take hold,
Cool fancies play, as glinting sunshine falls,

And the little child and his angel walk with God!
But ye fill all his days with paltry boons,
Poor thoughts, unworthy aims; that sacred place,
The altar of a child's pure heart, defile;
Thus ye despise the children.

Intrude not on his thoughts, his springs of love
And fear, the impulses that move, and all that store
He gathers to him to build his house of soul:
Let your communication be 'Yea, yea:
Nay, nay:' and let your 'yea' be full assured,
Your 'nay' be just and final: wary, walk warily,
Nor trespass on the child as were he clay
And you the forming potter: he is more;
See you, he comes with mind to comprehend;
With thoughts unformed, unplumbed, aware of all;
So filled with love from the pure Source, that toy
Of rag or stone or stick wakes tenderness,—
Behold, he hath transfigured the poor thing,
Made it yielding, loving, beauteous as himself!
Think you, he knows not God for he has no words
To tell you what he knows? E'en you, grown stale
In the world's uses, how can you discover
To any the deep thoughts which move you most?
Ye think him ignorant of right or wrong,
An unlettered sheet 'tis your part to inscribe?
On fleshly tablet are the commandments writ—
The child's obedient heart!
       See ye to it
That children are honoured 'mongst you; that I see,

At play in city streets, no little child
Made common by your usage,-hard and vain,
Wilful and greedy, loving but himself;—
Because ye say, forsooth, 'He is but small—
What matters aught a little child may do?'
Verily, it matters much; your Father wills
That all these little ones be kept in love
And guileless as he sent them;-souls uplift
To God as flowers uplift their face to the sun:
Not one would God have perish, learn deceit,
And that alien worship where He hath no place—
Self-consciousness, which hedgeth as a wall,
Shutting out God and life and needs of men!

I charge you, guard the little ones, and know,—
To keep them humble, innocent, as they grow,
Your chiefest care-task by the Father set!"

LXXII
Mother and Son (The disciple)

"These little ones which believe in Me."
"Little children... ye have known the Father."
"Out of the mouths of babes and sucklings hast Thou perfected
    praise."
"Their angels do always behold the face of My Father."

I

SHE sat at her young son's feet—
    Sat low by her sleeping boy—
Much pond'ring the high-born air he wore,
    As of native claim on joy.

"Sure not of his father or me
    Was he made thus free of the earth;
Ah, were we at large! but the hours confine,—
    Knows he a loftier birth?

"Great is the mystery! yea—
    How little, O babe, art thou mine!
A halo surrounds and divides thee,
    Living Words about thee shine!

"All faith and hide knowledge, thine—
 My little one, how can it be?
When sing'st thou those perfect praises—
 The Father, say, where dost see?

Thy Guardian waiteth ever
 On the face of our God for light,—
O little son, how high thy estate!
 Thy mother, alas, her plight!"

II

She slept. As one bends to waken
 A harp, so gave voice to her pain
The angel in ward: "Wherefore troubled?
 Thy boy's state, is it not all gain?"

"Yea, all my breath is thanksgiving,
 This heart lives in song for the grace;
Yet at moments a pang,—sure, not envy,—
 Comes with light on his face.

"To thine angel-state it were easy
 To win fullest thought of the Lord;
Faith comes to us wafted of storms: these—
 'Believe they on Me,' is his word!

"Say thou! These simple, how search they
   The mystery of things unseen?
By what wit can they know to trust Him
   Whose Name scarce lisp they, I ween?"

"Nay, mother, thy heart best answers;
   Is there any in all the wide land
So utterly trusts thee and worships,
   So keepeth him in thine hand,

"As the babe who not yet calls thee,
   Nor knows any name for his joy?
Thus it lies in the hand of the king,—
   The simple soul of thy boy!"

LXXIII

Letter to a child (The disciple)

MY news is of a King-a King so sweet
That might she place her low stool at His feet,
And sit and watch His face the live-long day,
"My happiest birthday this," would Susie say,
But that, for wisest reasons, may not be;
At least not yet. A mighty King is He,
And everything He wishes He can do;
So 'tis His pleasure oft to visit you,
And every little child whose name He knows.
But, that you may be in your weekday clothes,
And may behave as you do every day,
And not for company your best display,
He places His dear hand upon your eyes,
And holds them so-Tho' things of shape and size
You see quite well-you cannot tell when He
Is standing by, and so your thoughts are free,
And He sees just what kind of child you are.

But there is more to tell and better far:
You know He is a King; but, ah, not proud!
Not palace bright where many servants crowd

He chooses for his dwelling: the least room,
The tiniest house that anywhere may be,
A little maiden's heart, is not too wee
For Him to enter in and make His home.
You wonder that he can:-the King may come
Because He is so mighty, where He will:
And, if you watch for Him, your thoughts quite still,
You will find Some One good within your heart,
Who makes you care to choose the better part,
To be a gentle, thoughtful, loving child,
Not selfish, disobedient, cross, or wild.
And when He comes, he makes your face so fair,
Your friends are glad, and say, "The King is there!"

Page 183. No. 62

"Humility is one, in the same sense and truth as Christ is one, the Mediator is one, There are not two Lambs of God that take away the sins of the world. But if there was nay humility besides that of Christ, there would be something else besides Him that could take away the sins of the world."

WILLIAM LAW

BOOK II
SOME SAYINGS OF THE LORD'S

www.ingramcontent.com/pod-product-compliance
Lightning Source LLC
Chambersburg PA
CBHW070636170726
48291CB00003B/1033